Legacy in Legend

THUNDERSTONE

Book One

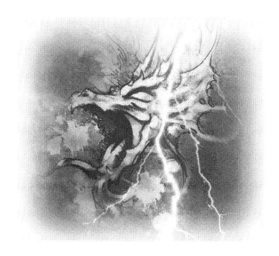

Barbara Pietron

Scribe Publishing Company
Royal Oak, Michigan

Legacy in Legend
Thunderstone
Book One

Published by Scribe Publishing Company
Royal Oak, Michigan
www.scribe-publishing.com

ISBN 978-1-940368-91-7

Printed in the U.S.

For Nikki—my inspiration, my toughest critic, and my biggest fan. Love you!

Humankind has not woven the web of life.
We are but one thread within it.
Whatever we do to the web, we do to ourselves.
All things are bound together.
All things connect.

—*Chief Seattle, Suquamish*

CHAPTER 1

Jeni was halfway back to the car when she heard the voice behind her.

"I'll double what you just paid for that statue."

She knew the offer was directed at her. She hadn't seen any other customers inside the convenience store where she'd just purchased a stone statue. And her cousin was the only one at the gas pumps. Still, she kept walking. Even quickened her pace a bit.

The scrape and crunch of gravel on her left warned of the guy's approach before she saw him from the corner of her eye.

"Excuse me. Uh… sorry to bother you, but the statue you just bought? I'd like to buy it. It's impor-tant," he babbled while shuffling alongside her. "Look, I'll give you forty bucks." The guy thrust his hand forward with two twenty-dollar bills sticking out.

Jeni's "stranger danger" reflex kicked her

heartbeat up a notch. She glanced sideways; surprised to see a young guy, seventeen or eighteen at most, with copper skin, black hair, and startling blue eyes. Her lips parted and her breath hitched involuntarily. Wow, the guy was super-cute.

Her feet slowed, though her pulse continued to race as a new nervous energy replaced her initial alarm. Maybe she should hear him out.

"Buzz off, buddy. Whatever you want to buy, she's not selling." Her cousin Tyler suddenly appeared in front of her, and Jeni stopped short to avoid running into him.

The guy raised his hands and held them out past his shoulders, the money still clenched in one fist. He gave Jeni a pleading look but took a step backward.

"Tyler, I... he just..."

Tyler grabbed Jeni's arm and propelled her toward the car. She shook off his hold on her. "What's your problem?"

"I saw him offering you money. Just get in and lock the door," he said. "I'll drive."

"Overreact much?" she muttered. Going back to talk to the guy now would be embarrassingly awkward, so Jeni got in the car. She was more than happy to let Tyler drive—it was better than him scrutinizing her newly-acquired driving skills—but he was acting like a jerk.

Not that that was new.

With the door closed, Jeni glanced in the side mirror and saw the guy hadn't moved. Dang. The well-worn jeans, athletic build, and sun-kissed skin added up to rugged hotness—the best kind of hotness in Jeni's opinion. Only his downcast expression was at odds with his outdoorsy brawn. A pang of sympathy struck her as he shook his head and scrubbed his hands over his face.

Tyler dropped into the driver's seat and slammed the door. "Um, maybe you should consider jeans that aren't quite so tight," he said. He started the car and pulled away from the pumps.

"What're you talk…" Jeni hissed out a disgusted sigh as she got his meaning. "You're such an idiot." She dug in the paper bag she'd set on the floor between her feet. After plunking two drinks into the cupholders, she drew out a small stone statue. "He wanted to buy this."

"How would I know that? A stranger waving money at a girl in a parking lot looks pretty suspicious to me. Besides, you went in to buy drinks."

"Puh-leeze, he was probably younger than you."

Tyler shrugged. "What is that anyway? A stone cat?"

"Well, it's not an ordinary cat, that's why I bought it." Jeni held the figure out. "Look, it has horns. And check this out, doesn't it look like it's painted with scales?"

Tyler glanced at the statue and grunted.

"The man at the store called it an artifact; maybe it's valuable. That guy offered me forty dollars and I only paid twelve," Jeni said.

"Try eBay. And I get a cut since I chased the dude off."

Jeni didn't dignify that with an answer. She might be twenty-eight dollars richer right now if Tyler hadn't chased the guy off. The cute guy. Tyler turned up the radio, and Jeni let her head fall back on the headrest. Trees and marsh flashed by on either side of the two-lane blacktop road. An occasional break in the foliage revealed dirt roads cutting through the woods, some which bore signs indicating residences beyond the dense vegetation. Jeni hardly noticed; she'd seen similar scenery back in Michigan—not where she lived in suburban Detroit, but a few hours north where her family went camping.

Something about the incident at the gas station didn't add up. She was pretty sure now that was the same guy she saw on the phone in the back room of the convenience store. At the time, she assumed he worked there. But if so, why would he rush out and try to buy the statue she just bought? It didn't make any sense.

Jeni could still picture his crestfallen face. He'd looked like a kid who had just dropped his science project and watched it explode into a million pieces.

She fingered the statue's cool, stone surface for a few moments, then slipped the figure into her pocket. The encounter definitely put a damper on her enthusiasm for the newest item in her cat collection. When she got back to civilization, she'd definitely Google 'cat with horns and scales' to see if anything came up.

As Tyler turned into Itasca State Park, Jeni thought about the beaded bracelet she'd returned to the rack after she spied the statue. She suddenly had the sinking feeling she would've been better off choosing the bracelet for a souvenir.

✱ ✱ ✱

"What happened? Where is it?"

Ice recoiled from the medicine man, thrusting the dance stick he'd purchased from Hoglund's Gas & Goods out in front of him.

The older man ignored the stick. "The statue. What did you do with the statue?"

"Nothing…I…I didn't get it."

"What do you mean you didn't get it?"

Ice backed up a step. He knew the medicine man would be disappointed, but he hadn't expected this kind of reaction. "Roffe sold it. While I was on the phone with you." He watched Nik pace the small room, his gray braid swinging outward each time the man spun on his heel. In the five years he'd studied with the medicine man, Ice had never seen him pace before.

"To who? Do you know? Did you see the person?"

"Yeah, some girl. Uh…Nik, I tried to buy it from her but when it looked like I'd have to fight her boy-friend, I backed off. You didn't sound too concerned over the phone."

"I wasn't concerned when we were on the phone, then—" Nik stepped around Ice to the doorway, peeked into the hall, then shut the door to his office. He motioned Ice to a seat then dropped into the chair behind his desk. "About five minutes ago I noticed a hawk. On my windowsill."

Ice raised his eyebrows.

The medicine man placed an object on the desk in front of his apprentice. "The bird left this behind."

Ice lifted what he at first thought was a rock. The smooth, dirty brown of one side contrasted with the varying shades of orange on the rough and crusty surface of the other side. Thinking back to some of the earliest lessons with the medicine man, Ice rubbed his thumb across a russet nodule and recognized a warm metallic element not present in stone. He met Nik's grave stare. "Copper."

Nik blew out a breath. "The omen couldn't be any plainer: copper delivered by a Thunderbird? Especially after you called about the statue…I was afraid you'd stopped somewhere close to water—too close."

Ice dropped his gaze to the floor. Uh-oh. He'd screwed up. Big time. "I'm sorry. I should've tried harder to get the statue from that girl. I should—"

"Ice," Nik interrupted. "It's not your fault. I told Roffe to go ahead and sell the figures. He listed them over the phone yesterday. I just wasn't thinking when he said 'cat'."

Nik's assurances didn't have much of an effect. Ice had been in the store; he knew the statue depicted the underwater monster, Mishebeshu. He should've gotten the figure from Roffe first and then called Nik.

A few years back, Nik had revealed the truth about the artifacts he collected: authentic relics used in rituals and ceremonies maintain their connection to the spirit world. That connection could be tapped by anyone with the requisite ancestry. The danger was twofold: for a person who knew their own potential, the spiritual link could be harnessed for selfish and often unethical purposes; for the person unaware of their dormant capability, the accidental contact could prove disastrous.

"The question is," Nik said, leaning back in his chair, "did the Thunderbird warn about the statue or about the underwater manitou himself? If the statue is our only concern, and the girl who bought it simply sits it on a shelf, we might be okay."

Ice stayed quiet, allowing the medicine man to sort out his thoughts.

"We need answers. I prefer to be proactive considering the potential threat posed by the underwater monster, so I'll go to the vision quest lodge and see what I can learn from the spirit world." Nik's gaze settled on Ice. "Is there any chance you could find this girl?"

Ice started to shake his head then froze. "Maybe."

✳ ✳ ✳

"How'd the drive go?" Jeni's mom asked.

"How do you think it went?" Jeni grumbled, holding her hands up and glowering at the drips accumulating on the kitchen floor. Her jacket and shirt, wet from the waist down, hung limply over her waterlogged jeans.

"What happened?"

"Tyler. That's what happened." Jeni kicked off her shoes and tromped to the bathroom. She peeled off her wet jacket and began to twist it into a bundle. With a heavy sigh she paused, extracted the bizarre cat statue from her pocket, then wrung the jacket over the tub. If today was an indication of what this family gathering would be like, it was going to be a long, miserable week.

"What?" she barked in response to a knock on the door.

"Do you want me to bring you some dry clothes?" her mom asked.

Since she could hardly traipse around in her underwear with thirteen other people in the cabin, Jeni told her mom which clothes she wanted. When her mom returned, she offered to wring out Jeni's jeans.

"I told you Tyler always thinks I'm around for his amusement," Jeni said. "That's why I didn't want to go with him in the first place." She rubbed her legs with a towel. "You know why he asked me to drive?"

"So you could practice maybe? Or to give you guys something to do?"

"No. His car's a stick. He wanted to laugh at me." Her mom didn't get it. She seemed to think cousins were automatically friends.

"Well, the joke was on him then, right? Since you know how to drive one."

Uh-uh. She was not going to let her mom put a positive spin on this. "I hope you brought Band-Aids. I'm bleeding." Jeni dabbed her ankle with toilet tissue.

Her mom rifled through the toiletries bag. "How did you do that?"

"On a rock. When I fell in the water. We went to Itasca State Park, figured we'd check out the Mississippi Headwaters so we'd know what to expect when we… do the grandpa thing." Remembering their purpose here in northern Minnesota dampened Jeni's urge to take out her frustration on her mom. She dropped an octave of venom from her voice as she explained that the headwaters of the Mississippi—which looked more like a creek than a river—were marked by a row of large rocks. Tyler crossed them easily and challenged her to do the same. It didn't go as well for Jeni.

"Look honey, it's a family trip. And I realize everyone here is either an adult or a toddler, except for you." Her mom picked up the Band-Aid tabs and threw them in the trash. "It seems like you get stuck hanging out with adults all the time. It's been that way since you were a baby. So I'm sorry if I pushed you into the ride with Tyler, but he's at least close to your age and I figured you were both old enough to get along."

"Mom, even when I'm an old lady Tyler will try to make me look stupid so he can laugh at me."

"I doubt that. He didn't laugh when you fell, did he?"

"Pretty much…well, not at first." Jeni frowned. "I probably had a strange look on my face because when I sat down in the water I went all woozy—like I was going to pass out." She slid her legs into the dry jeans and then stood to pull them up.

"The water was that cold?"

"No. I mean, it was cold, but not that bad. A shock to the system I would've expected. The dizziness was weird. As soon as I got on my feet though, I felt better." Jeni shrugged. "Anyway, once he saw I was okay, Tyler felt free to smirk."

Jeni's mom stuffed the box of bandages back into the satchel. "I'm sure he wouldn't want to hurt you—or see you get hurt. You do realize he teases you because he likes you? If he didn't like you he'd just ignore you."

Jeni moved in front of the mirror and rolled her eyes at her reflection. Even if it was true, it didn't make the teasing any easier to bear. Her mom shifted so their eyes met in the mirror. "Honey, Tyler just treats you like a sister. Now you know what it's like to have a brother."

"Yeah, it's fabulous," Jeni muttered, though the dry clothes were already improving her mood. She picked up a hairbrush and ran it through her hair.

"You may feel differently in ten years or so." Her mom reached for the doorknob. "I better finish slicing the tomatoes. I bet the hamburgers are about ready," she said as she stepped into the hallway.

"Mom?" Jeni waited until her mom poked her head back in the room. "You should have seen Tyler's face when I backed up his car and drove it through the resort. It was priceless. He definitely wasn't expecting that from a girl with a learner's permit."

Her mom grinned. "See? I knew learning to drive a stick would come in handy."

"Yeah, yeah." Jeni waved her off with a slight smile.

She put down the brush and stared at her reflection. Even though her mom encouraged the drive with Tyler, it wasn't her fault Jeni fell in the water. It wasn't even Tyler's fault—as much as she wanted to blame him. No, it was her own fault.

She'd listened to his assurances; let him convince her when she knew better.

Hadn't she learned her lesson in third grade? Never trust a boy.

* * *

Ice felt like an idiot sitting in his car monitoring visitors to the Headwaters Center. The cup of coffee he sipped didn't help. All he needed was a doughnut or some kind of fast food sandwich to complete the stereotypical picture of a stakeout. When he'd agreed to apprentice the medicine man, Ice never imagined surveillance would be among his duties.

But he had only one lead to the girl who bought the statue at Hoglund's Gas & Goods yesterday. As he'd entered the store from the stock room, he heard her tell Roffe she'd be visiting the headwaters the next morning.

This morning.

Although Ice arrived before the first employee showed up to open the Center, his wasn't the first car in the lot. Dedicated exercisers preferred vacant trails. So far, Ice had watched two joggers finish their daily trek and move on.

He slumped in his seat as a truck entered the parking area. It wasn't the vehicle from the gas pumps yesterday; still, Ice studied the people inside. He wasn't going to chance missing the girl.

About an hour later, he regretted drinking coffee but maintained his post.

Another thirty minutes and seven cars later, a sedan followed by a pick-up truck wheeled into the lot. Two more cars trailed behind. Ice tracked a silver hatchback with interest. All four vehicles parked in a cluster and as people piled out, he had a difficult time picking out who emerged from which vehicle.

Not that it mattered. The honey-blonde hair was a dead giveaway. This morning the girl wore it loose, where yesterday it was in a ponytail, but Ice had no doubt about her identity. The large group unloaded various items and started for the trail. When the last person disappeared into the forest, Ice got out and followed.

The overnight chill still lingered among the trees. The swish of feet through last fall's leaves accompanied hushed conversation from the people ahead. Ice's churning stomach made him glad he hadn't eaten yet. How would he nonchalantly approach her? She'd think he was some kind of creepy stalker.

Ice hung back as the group reached a clearing. They stood staring up at a tree stump about ten feet tall. A flat, notched out portion served as a sign which read in bright yellow letters:

*HERE 1475 FT ABOVE THE OCEAN THE
MIGHTY MISSISSIPPI BEGINS TO
FLOW ON ITS WINDING WAY 2552
MILES TO THE GULF OF MEXICO*

Beyond the sign, the waters of Lake Itasca rippled in the cool morning breeze. To the right, the lake spilled over a trail of sizable rocks crossing a span of water: the Mississippi Headwaters.

The group didn't linger however; they filed down a side trail which led to a bridge about thirty feet downstream. Seats built into the bridge's side rails provided a place to set their various bags and coolers. Ice preferred to approach the girl when she was more sequestered from the group, so he left the path and melded with the trees to watch and wait.

Great. Now he felt like a creepy stalker.

Included in their provisions was a boom box, and soon music wafted across the marshy area. Horns. Jazz. The song wasn't quite "When the Saints Go Marching In," but the tune was similar. Next, Ice heard the unmistakable pop of a beverage can. He looked on with some amusement when he recognized cans of beer. Others held out cups to be filled with wine. What was going on here? Some kind of celebration?

Ice stepped a bit closer, careful to stay concealed.

As one of the men squatted down with a plastic bag and tilted the opening over the edge of the planking, Ice got it.

Ashes.

These people were here to spread someone's ashes in the Mississippi Headwaters.

Ice didn't make a conscious decision—he simply knew he couldn't approach the girl here. As important as his mission was, his respect for one's journey into the afterlife prevailed.

He'd have to come up with a Plan B.

A danger foreseen is half-avoided.

—Cheyenne Proverb

CHAPTER 2

The breeze lifted Jeni's hair and draped it over her face. Shivering, she tucked a lock behind her ear. Summer had yet to spread its full-blown warmth to northern Minnesota. The sun had slipped behind the cottage while she read, casting the deck into shade. The beach, however, remained in full sunlight. With the next gust of wind Jeni set aside her copy of Bram Stoker's *Dracula* and abandoned her chair. Warm sunshine enveloped her as she walked along the edge of the lake collecting good skipping stones. When she couldn't fit anymore in her hand, she began throwing them, counting the number of skips.

"Wow, five, that's pretty good."

Jeni jumped. Without turning her head, she caught a glimpse of a guy standing on her right. Most likely someone from one of the other cottages. Wonderful— she should've stayed in her chair. "Thanks," she muttered and continued to throw.

To her dismay, he began collecting stones. His first few throws barely grazed the water before sinking. "How do you make them skip so many times?" he asked.

Jeni had planned to finish throwing the rocks in her hand and get the heck out of there. She had no interest in some strange guy saying stupid things or trying to impress her. But she'd been taught not to be rude, and he'd asked her a direct and harmless question, so she opened her fist and showed him the two stones she had left. "They have to be kinda flat, like this."

His black hair brushed the tops of his shoulders as he bent forward to collect stones of a similar shape. Despite the cool breeze, he wore a t-shirt, which exposed tanned skin. Something in her brain clicked, but before she made the connection, he stood and held out his hand. "Like these?"

She instinctively looked into his face first and for a moment was rendered speechless. Jeni dropped her remaining rocks on the sand.

It was the guy from the convenience store yesterday.

"Don't go, please," he said, reading her stance and probably the suspicion on her face as well. "I want to apologize for yesterday...and explain if you'll let me."

"How did...did you follow me?" Jeni glanced at the cottage to see if anyone was around. Tyler's dad stood on the side deck smoking a cigarette. Good.

"I...I do odd jobs here at the resort. I thought I recognized you. Listen, I know I probably freaked you out yesterday and I'm sorry. But I'm not a creep," he hurried to explain.

What freaked her out was his showing up here. But he sounded...sincere. And she was curious. She folded her arms and didn't say anything.

He met her gaze directly and she was struck again by his appearance. His eyes were impossibly blue, the irises broken into mosaic-like fragments. His scrutiny made her feel as if he saw more of her than just her outward appearance. Jeni wasn't sure if that was a good thing or a bad thing.

"A man who collects Native American artifacts sent me to the store. I was on the phone with him when you came in. It just so happened that you bought the same item he was interested in. I panicked. I didn't know how he'd react if I came back without it."

"Why? Is it worth a lot of money or something?"

The guy smiled, his thoughts unreadable. "Or something. He's Indian so these things have more value to him than to others. To him, some are priceless."

"And my statue is one of them?"

"I think so."

"Oh." If what he said was true, Jeni felt kind of bad about the situation. Did this man have more right to the statue than she did?

The guy threw another one of the stones he'd picked up. It smacked the surface of the water and sank.

Jeni said, "It's not just the shape."

"What?"

"The stones. It's not just the shape; it's also how you throw them." She retrieved one of the rocks she'd dropped, positioned it between her fingers and thumb, then drew her arm down underhanded and flicked her wrist. The rock sailed over the water and bounced off the surface three times.

He mimicked her motion and also got three skips. "Cool. Thanks." He tossed another. "So are you here on vacation?" he asked.

Good grief, now she'd done it—promoted a conversation. She'd merely wanted to know what was up with the statue.

"Kinda." She wouldn't exactly call this trip a vacation.

He threw again. Four skips.

Though he didn't ask, Jeni felt compelled to explain. "It's a family gathering."

Finished with his stones, he brushed his hands on his jeans. "By the way, I'm Ice."

Ice? Seriously? Was this guy for real? Still, her automatic reaction to an introduction had already kicked in. "Jeni," she heard herself say. Her eyes darted to his for a second, her stomach flipped, and she looked away. Dang, he was good-looking.

"Yeah, yeah, I know I have an unusual name. There're a lot of unusual names around here." He flashed a smile and stuffed his hands in his pockets. "As you probably guessed, I'm Native American— Ojibwe—well, mostly, everything but the eyes." He laughed nervously, and when Jeni didn't reply, he jabbered on, determined to fill the conversational gap. "Actually, my eyes are how I got my name. My full name is Shattered Ice, but everyone just calls me Ice."

His explanation made sense. Jeni figured she should either join the conversation or make an excuse to leave. As much as the latter appealed to her, she wondered why he hadn't asked again to buy her statue. "Do you live around here?"

Ice shuffled his feet around at the water's edge, using the toe of his sneaker to turn rocks over. "About a half hour away, in Cass Lake. How about you?" He selected a stone and threw it. Four skips.

"I'm from Michigan."

"I've been to Michigan. Charlevoix."

"I live on the other side of the state—near Detroit."

"Wow, long way for a family gathering." Ice fired a stone that skittered across the water. Jeni counted at least six skips.

"Yeah, well, this is where the Mississippi Headwaters are." Rather than get into a conversation about the reason for this particular destination, Jeni decided to get to the point. "So…what are you waiting for?"

He turned to her. "What?"

"Do you still want to buy that statue?"

"Do you want to sell it?"

Answer a question with a question—two could play that game. "Isn't that why you're here?"

Ice shrugged. "I didn't want you to think I was a psycho. I prefer to be straight with people."

Jeni watched as his next stone skimmed the water's surface and bounced five times. "Like you were straight with me when you pretended you didn't know how to skip stones?"

"Uh…" Ice muttered a weak protest. The corners of his mouth barely twitched, though he couldn't keep the smile from his eyes.

Jeni should've been angry—she wanted to be

angry. Using some kind of ruse to talk to a girl was such a typical guy maneuver. But Ice's sheepish expression had the same effect as a puppy sitting among the ruins of a pillow and looking up with large innocent eyes. Jeni chuckled. "You live in an area where you can hardly step out your front door without walking into a lake and you expect me to believe you don't know how to skip stones?"

"Well, I do now." His wide grin softened the lines of his cheekbones and Jeni's heartbeat seemed to stumble for a moment.

"Okay Mr. 'I prefer to be straight with people', what can you tell me about my statue?" The shade had worked its way down the lawn and across the beach. Jeni pulled the zipper up on her hoodie and put her hands in the pockets.

"Sun's still on the dock," Ice pointed out.

Jeni nodded. As she sat down on the warm wood and crossed her legs in front of her, she wondered what Ice was really doing here. People don't care that much about a brief encounter to seek out a stranger and apologize, right? Regardless, she no longer felt weirded out, and as long as he was here she might as well find out why a cat would have scales and horns.

* * *

Ice followed Jeni onto the dock. He was totally winging it. That's what Plan B consisted of: trusting his instincts. His heartbeat, which had almost regulated after throwing rocks, picked up pace as he watched

Jeni's slim figure turn and sit down on the dock. Her blonde hair glimmered in the setting sun. She absently brushed it back from her face and glanced back at him.

This would be easier if she wasn't so pretty.

When he'd looked deep in her eyes he sensed a sort of…kinship…that unnerved him. Did Jeni possess an inborn link to the spirit world? Nik believed the gift was more common than anyone suspected; most people just weren't in tune to such things these days and often spent a lifetime unaware of their ability. But the thunderbird presented the copper to Nik for a reason. And the only way Ice could know for sure if Jeni was able to commune with the world beyond was to touch her. The thought made his stomach burn.

He dropped down next to her. "Actually, your statue is a revered figure in Ojibwe mythology."

"It is?" She sounded genuinely interested— excited even. From the corner of his eye, Ice could see the smile on her face. "So I could probably find stories about it? I love myths and legends. Dragons, wizards, gods and goddesses, vampires…all that stuff."

"Mmmm, I happen to know quite a few legends about the Underwater Lynx."

Jeni groaned. She turned toward Ice, but her eyes were on the cottage. He glanced over his shoulder. "Uh-oh." He'd forgotten about the boyfriend.

The guy stood on the deck, arms crossed, seem-ingly scanning the horizon, though markedly avoid-ing the figures on the dock. Ice guessed the dude was a few years older and a couple inches taller than him.

"My cousin. Just ignore him."

"Your cousin?"

Jeni rolled her eyes. "Yeah, and he'll probably tease me mercilessly—especially if he recognizes you from yesterday."

"Uh...sorry."

"Whatever. He always finds a way to pick on me." Then Jeni smiled. "If you told me a legend, though, it would be worth it."

Ice should've been relieved to know the guy was only her cousin, but instead his nerves ratcheted up a notch. Suddenly Jeni wasn't part of a couple; she was a girl. And he didn't have the best track record when it came to the opposite sex. It seemed he never knew the right things to say and do—or maybe he just attracted the wrong kind of girls—because they inevitably lost interest. Taking a deep breath, Ice reminded himself that his purpose here had nothing to do with making a good impression.

Besides, right now he did have Jeni's interest. "What did you call it? An underwater lion?" she asked.

He smiled. "Lynx—not lion. His name is Mishebeshu, although most Indians call him the Underwater Manitou—or spirit. He's the most feared monster in American Indian legend; catching people when they least expect him. His choice of time, place, and victim is totally random."

Jeni paid rapt attention, so Ice continued. "He'd cause dangerous rapids on rivers to overturn canoes or make whirlwinds on the surface of lakes to cause people to drown."

Her eyes were wide, but her forehead wrinkled. "If it's a water monster, why a cat? And what's up with the horns and scales?"

Ice shrugged. "Cats are known for stealth, that

would be my guess. The horns and scales are said to be made of copper, a valuable medicine. Sometimes the manitou would let medicine men collect the copper, but at a high price. They usually paid with the lives of their children or wife."

Jeni didn't reply, her gaze once again on the cottage. "My dad," she muttered. "What do you want to bet Tyler sent him out here?"

Neither spoke as they watched Jeni's father approach. When he was close enough, Jeni called out, "Hi, Dad." She gave him a little wave. "This is Ice. He's going to tell me an Ojibwe legend."

Jeni's father strode purposefully onto the dock. "I'll bet," he said.

"What?" Jeni looked up at him.

"I said I'll bet he knows a lot of legends."

Ice stuck out his hand, willing it to remain steady. "Nice to meet you."

"Yes, it is," Jeni's dad agreed. He shook Ice's hand with a bemused expression and then contemplated the boat. "I'm going fishing with Tyler in the morning and I wanted to see if the oars were already out here."

Ice met Jeni's eyes. She gave a slight shrug. "Will you tell me a legend about the Underwater Lynx?"

"Well—

"Better make it a short 'scary tale', they're almost ready to eat in there," Jeni's dad interrupted, pointing up to the cabin.

"Dad!" Jeni rolled her eyes. "They're legends, not fairy tales!"

Once her dad was out of earshot, Jeni looked at

Ice apologetically. "My dad loves to be the wise guy. He kinda prides himself on it."

"Yeah, I got that." Ice smiled to cover his alarm that she might go in for dinner before he figured out how to touch her casually. A stupid move could easily undo his efforts to convince her he was harmless. "Sounds like there's not time for a story about your statue."

"You don't know a short one?

"Not with the Underwater Manitou." Ice cast a sidelong glance at Jeni and noticed her studying the remnants of the sun slanting through the trees. She peered anxiously around her. "I should get going anyway."

Ice scrambled to buy a little more time. "How about the legend of Lake Itasca? You came here to see the headwaters and the story is super short."

"Okay." Jeni leaned back on her hands.

Ice began without preamble. "Nanabushu, a demi-god sent to protect the people, had a beautiful daughter named Itasca. The ruler of the underworld, Chebiabo, fell madly in love with Itasca. He wanted her to marry him and live in the underworld.

"Itasca didn't want to leave the magnificence of earth to go live in the dark. Her response infuriated Chebiabo. He raged, causing a huge storm that swept Itasca below the earth. Now she mourns for the world above, and her tears are the springs that trickle to the lake and form the source of the Mississippi River."

Jeni's face brightened. "It reminds me of the story of Persephone."

"Persephone?" It was now or never. Ice leaned

back and 'accidentally' put his hand on Jeni's. A slight hum or vibration flowed through his hand and up his arm—as if a small, motorized appliance sat on the deck with them. He watched her face closely, his heart sinking as her eyes went wide and unseeing.

"Ooops, sorry," he mumbled and removed his hand.

A hollow ache of guilt settled in Ice's chest at Jeni's dumbstruck look of confusion. He remembered the strange visions that flickered to life in his head when Nik first took his hand—except Ice had had some idea that it might happen; he knew Nik was testing him to see if he could touch the spirit world. Jeni obviously had no clue she possessed such a gift. He picked up the conversation, trying to smooth over the disruption. "Isn't Persephone from Greek mythology?"

"Yeah…uh…yeah." Jeni blinked. "Sorry, I lost my train of thought for a minute. Let's see…Hades—ruler of the underworld—falls in love with Persephone, brings her to the underworld and marries her." Ice followed Jeni's lead when she stood and brushed sand from her jeans. "At first she won't eat, but Hades talks her into eating four pomegranate seeds."

She set off at a brisk pace and Ice lengthened his strides in order to stay next to her while she finished her story.

"Anyway, Persephone does get returned to earth, but because she ate the seeds she always has to return to the underworld for four months. It's how the Greeks explained the seasons. When Persephone's in the upper world it's growing season and when she's in the underworld the earth is barren."

As soon as she reached the circle of the cottage's floodlight, Jeni slowed and dropped her shoulders with a small sigh.

"The stories are kinda similar," Ice said.

Jeni nodded, pausing a few feet from the deck stairs. "I think a lot of myths are."

They stood there for an awkward long second. The brightly lit kitchen window gave them an alternative to looking at each other, and they watched as Jeni's family members trickled into the room.

"I guess I better go in," Jeni said. But instead of turning toward the steps, she studied him for a moment with a mildly furrowed brow. "Did you catch a lot of flack about not getting the statue?"

Ice had a quick debate on how to answer her question. The artifact in her hands had the potential of a gas can near a fire. On the other hand, judging by her reaction to his touch, she was unaware of her abilities. Maybe sitting on a bedroom shelf was the safest place for such a thing. Although he couldn't let her keep it without some kind of warning. "No," he answered, the corners of his mouth twitching upward. "Only a little flack." Jeni smiled—exactly the reaction he'd hoped for. He wanted to keep the conversation light. Returning her smile he said, "But now that you know what the statue is, don't take it to the beach or anything."

Jeni giggled. "Too late. I already went swimming with it."

"Yeah, right." Ice chuckled, but he didn't like the way she'd blushed as she said it. She couldn't be serious?

Jeni rolled her eyes and the color in her cheeks deepened. "Well, I didn't take it swimming so much as dunked it in the water." She looked at the grass. "I fell in the water trying to cross the stones at the headwaters. The statue was in my pocket."

Ice barely caught the rest of her story as his mind reeled. Oh god, no. The statue…Jeni…in the water together…was it enough to get the Underwater Monster's attention?

"…okay. Just a little scrape on the ankle."

Great. Even better. She bled in the water. She might as well have scratched her name in the sand with directions on how to find her.

He suddenly realized Jeni had stopped speaking and regarded him expectantly. He attempted a chuckle that sounded more like he was choking. "Yeah…uh… people fall there all the time."

Apparently his reply sufficed because Jeni smiled up at him shyly. "Too bad we didn't have time for a legend about the Underwater Lynx." She made her way to the bottom of the deck stairs and stood with her hand on the rail. "Uh…maybe if you're around another day?"

The suggestion took Ice by surprise until it dawned on him that she probably thought he worked at the resort. "Yeah," he blurted. "I'll be around."

"Well…if you have time…"

"Sure. I guess I'll probably see you…later then."

He waited until Jeni was at the cottage door. She turned and waved.

Ice raised his hand briefly then walked off into the dark. Holy crap. His pulse pounded in his ears. If he'd known about Jeni's fall in the river, he'd have responded differently when she asked about the statue. He could have told her he caught a lot of flack. That he'd still like to—no, needed to—buy the statue from her.

He took a deep breath, trying to convince himself he was overreacting. He didn't *know* anything had happened. Mishebeshu hadn't been a threat to the people for over a hundred years; surely there was a chance the omen Nik received had nothing to do with Jeni.

But in his heart, his arguments fell flat.

Life is simple. Man complicates it.

—Edna Gordon, Seneca

CHAPTER 3

Nothing happened quickly with fourteen people staying in the same cottage. Especially not shower rotations. Fortunately, Jeni started the habit of showering at night when she'd started high school and had the bathroom to herself last night—with no one waiting at the door. So while most of the family vied for bathroom time, Jeni volunteered to help her aunt with breakfast.

"How many eggs?" she asked Tyler's mom.

"I don't know when your dad and Tyler will be back so don't count them; and Josie doesn't eat eggs."

"Me neither."

"Okay then…" her aunt ticked off her fingers. "The little ones won't eat much either—let's just go with a dozen. It's easy enough to scramble more."

"All right." Jeni began breaking eggs into a bowl.

"Wow, that's impressive," her aunt commented. "You don't eat eggs but you can crack them one handed?"

"Yeah," Jeni said, pleased that her aunt had noticed. "I love to bake." She found a whisk and lightly beat the eggs.

Nearly forty-five minutes later they were gathered around the table, finally having breakfast at 10:00 a.m. They planned to go to the park today, but no one was in a hurry.

"Nat and I were talking about going to the playground after breakfast," announced Jeni's aunt, who had a three-year-old son. "Everyone is welcome to join us."

"I'll go," Jeni said. She'd been looking for an excuse to get outside. She didn't want to admit it— even to herself—but she wondered if Ice was at the resort already.

She still hoped to see him today despite the razzing she'd taken last night at dinner. Tyler, of course, started it by asking if she always talked to strange stalker guys. He ignored her attempt to explain. When one of her aunts tried to defend her by commenting, "Jeni can't help it if she's hot," Jeni cleared her plate and fled to the safety of the bathroom. After a long shower, she read and listened to her iPod, falling asleep at a relatively early hour.

Consequently, she'd woken up early this morning and heard someone already up and about. Jeni checked the time: 6:45, then remembered her dad and Tyler were going fishing. Hopefully they'd leave soon.

Careful not to disturb her grandma in the neighboring bed, Jeni donned a pair of jeans and pulled a sweatshirt on over her pajama top. About ten minutes later, the rumble of the sliding door announced the fishermen's departure. She waited another minute, listening to the silence of the sleeping dwelling, and then slipped from the room.

From the kitchen window, she confirmed Tyler and her dad were in the boat. As soon as they rowed away from the dock, Jeni put on shoes and a fleece jacket—it would be chilly out at 7:00 a.m.

Huddled on the dock, Jeni smiled grimly as the bars appeared on her cell phone display. It sucked that she had to sit out here even to text. Talk about the boonies. She'd counted on conversations with her best friend, Carolyn, to get her through the evenings. But once it got dark out, Jeni wasn't about to wander out to the dock by herself.

Now she was worried about running out of books to read and was reduced to this: trying to catch Carolyn before and after work. Her friend had scored a job at a YMCA summer camp for elementary school kids.

You up? She typed.

The reply didn't take long. *Yes unfortunately* ☹

Remember the cute guy who wanted to buy the statue I bought the day we got here? He showed up at the resort last night.

What the heck? Is he stalking you?

Not really. He apologized for freaking me out. He's actually pretty nice.

Jeni lifted her face to the warm sun that had finally peeked through the tops of the trees. When Carolyn didn't reply immediately, Jeni figured she must be brushing her teeth or was possibly interrupted by her mom or one of her annoying little brothers. A couple minutes later, Jeni's phone buzzed.

Nice because he still wants your souvenir?

I don't think so. He didn't ask me for it again.

So he's just hot for you lol

Ha ha. He just felt bad.

That's all he said?

No. He told me he's Native American and somehow we ended up talking about legends and myths

Jeni could've guessed what her friend's comment would be; Carolyn knew Jeni well. She smiled as she read the reply, *So he's a geek like you* ☺ *maybe you met your soulmate What's his name?*

Yeah right lol. You're gonna be all over this but remember he's Indian. His name is Shattered Ice and he goes by just Ice

I guess I can accept that since he's Indian—and cute :D Will you see him again?

Maybe today.

You better fill me in on all the details later. Btw did Tyler ask about me lol

Carolyn made fun of her own question, but Jeni knew there was a modicum of actual curiosity there. When she'd introduced her friend to Tyler at her grandpa's funeral, Carolyn's reaction was unmistakable; subtle, but something a best friend picked up on immediately. Actually, it was the first time Jeni had ever considered Tyler's appearance from a girl's perspective. He was her *cousin.* And he was annoying.

He probably doesn't even remember your name—no fault of yours, he's just an idiot most of the time. You can do better The thought of Tyler dating her best friend made Jeni shudder. Thank goodness he lived in Wisconsin.

Gotta take off. My mom's letting me drive.

Ok. Have a good one

Jeni clicked her phone off and sighed. She needed more time to talk to her friend. She didn't even have time to tell Carolyn about the strange episode she had on the dock last night when she was talking to Ice. She'd just started telling him about Persephone when her vision went black for a second and flames materialized, flickering in the darkness. Then, beyond the flames, silhouettes swayed…to drums. Drum beats pulsed from within her.

Then she was looking at the lake again. The episode freaked her out. Nothing like that had ever happened to her before. She didn't have time to dwell on the strange incident since Ice prompted her by asking if Persephone was from Greek mythology. Too embarrassed to tell him what had happened (since she didn't even know what happened), she managed to recover and finish the story. Later, in bed, she went over the scene in her mind, trying to pinpoint what might've made her 'black out', but she'd come up with nothing.

Finally she chalked it up to all of the unfamiliar stimuli, not sleeping well in a strange bed, and the talk of myths and legends.

"Looks like Tyler and your dad are back from fishing," Tyler's mom commented, snapping Jeni back to the present. She was glad she'd volunteered to go to the playground because another good reason to leave the cabin had just arrived at the dock. "Is he done?" she asked Nat's mom.

"I think so. So am I."

Jeni stacked up their plates and carried them to the sink. Checking out the window, she saw Tyler tying up the boat while her dad transferred tackle to the dock.

Jeni's aunt finished tying Nat's shoes and noticed Jeni hovering at the window. "Go get your jacket," she told her son, then met Jeni's eyes. "We can meet you outside, if you want."

Jeni smiled. "Great." She grabbed her jacket and slipped out the side door just as her dad and Tyler reached the deck.

Her number one objective for the day was to avoid Tyler like the plague.

* * *

Ice slept in. Not on purpose, he'd had a hard time getting to sleep last night. When he did finally drift off, strange dreams resulted in a restless slumber. Knowing vision quests take time, Ice hadn't gone straight from the resort to the lodge; figuring talking to the medicine man last night wouldn't have changed anything

In retrospect though, perhaps getting everything off his chest would've allowed him a good night's sleep.

The sharp aroma of coffee got him out of bed and into the kitchen. His mom always turned the coffee maker off before she left, but the pot was still warm. He poured a cup and brought it in the bathroom with him.

Ice tried to get his thoughts in order while he showered. Aside from the things he needed to tell Nik, he had questions as well. But by the time he climbed in his Jeep, his own conjecture was driving him crazy. To preserve his sanity, he cranked up the music on his way to Knutson Dam Campground.

He parked in the campground day-use lot and set out on foot for the isolated lodge overlooking Cass Lake. As the path drew parallel to the beach, Ice spotted the gray, domed roof protruding from the long beach grass. Fashioned from curved boughs covered with birch bark, the lodge easily masqueraded as a large boulder.

The waves lapped softly at the sand and a seagull cried in the distance. He padded forward, distributing his weight on the balls of his feet.

"Come in, Ice."

Ice ducked under the hide hanging in the hut's doorway. "You heard me?"

"Here," Nik said and pointed to his head. "Sensed you coming. Kind of like knowing someone is on the other end of the phone line even if they don't speak."

Ice still struggled to fully develop that capability. He received mental communication from the medicine man, and could sense Nik in his head, but only just before a message came through. Sending an answer in return had proved problematic.

"It'll come," Nik said, reading the look on his apprentice's face. "Perhaps when technology fails you, you'll make the connection."

Since the lodge had been the location of his initial vision quest, Ice knew the interior lacked creature comforts. Devoid of furniture, the small dwelling offered only shelter and existed for one purpose: serenity. Nik motioned to the ground next to him. "Sit. Your anxiety entered before you did. Tell me what you know."

"I found the girl." Ice rushed the words out, glad to share the burden. "When I spoke to her, I perceived a kind of…connection just by looking her in the eyes. Eventually I managed to casually touch her hand and felt a bond—different than ours though. Maybe because she's a girl? Anyway, the thought that came to me was 'priestess'."

He paused to give the medicine man a chance to comment. Lines creased Nik's forehead, but he remained silent. Ice rubbed at a clump of sand stuck to the side of his shoe and reluctantly continued. "There's more. And I think it's pretty bad." He raised his chin. "She fell in the river. She had the statue in her pocket."

Nik closed his eyes and exhaled heavily. "When?"

"Right after she bought it."

"Same time as the omen."

Ice nodded. He'd thought it over last night and deduced the same thing.

"We have to assume the Underwater Manitou has been roused—thus, the warning. It's up to us, then, to subdue him before he escapes his prison."

"I don't understand," Ice said. "In the legends, Mishebeshu is in the Great Lakes—not the river. Besides, how could this happen now? After a hundred years?"

Ice fought the urge to squirm as he felt Nik's gaze evaluating him.

"You're right, Ice. When the world was made, the Underwater Manitou inhabited the Great Lakes. Some inland lakes also were suspected to be linked as part of an underground tunnel system the creature traveled. Our people didn't fish certain lakes because of the unnatural color of the water and reports of sightings or incidents that occurred there. But the big water was most dangerous. Unfortunately, newcomers to our land have always seen fit to disturb the environment if it benefits them. Have you heard of the Illinois Waterway?"

Ice shook his head.

"The Great Lakes and the Mississippi watershed don't have a natural connection." Nik emphasized the word "natural." "Over one hundred and fifty years ago Congress authorized a canal that would connect Lake Michigan to the Illinois River. It was finished in the mid 1800's—even reversing the flow of the Chicago River to accomplish the feat.

"Not long after that our people witnessed signs of the manitou in the rivers. It started with bad fishing, but soon people were dying; overturned canoes, children drawn under by whirlpools. The visions of the elders agreed: the Great Spirit was angry; things were not how they'd been created. Unable to do anything about the canal, the medicine men of neighboring tribes joined together to lure the creature here. They trapped him in a cavern near the sacred burial mounds of Lake Itasca and charmed him to sleep."

Nik gazed in the direction of Lake Itasca as if he could see the site. "Two braves gave their lives to guard the opening. One of them is my great-great grandfather." He paused for a moment of respectful silence and then continued the narrative. "So my ancestors have kept watch, passing the responsibility from generation to generation. Some of the burial mounds were discovered and excavated years ago, but the cavern and its guards remained intact."

"If the monster somehow escapes the guards, he'll exact his vengeance—no waters will be safe." Nik locked eyes with his apprentice as if to make sure he understood the gravity of his words. "We'll need the statue to reverse what's happened."

Ice nodded once in assent; another conclusion he'd drawn while lying awake last night. He didn't move to leave. Instead, he flicked another clump of sand from his shoe, mulling over an internal debate.

"Ice? Is there something else?"

Ice glanced up. "It's probably nothing. I had a dream last night with Jeni in it."

"The girl who bought the statue?"

"Yeah. Her name's Jeni."

"Tell me."

"Well, we were at a lake skipping stones. Jeni became anxious—and confused. She said she heard drumming and kept asking me, "Can't you hear the drums?" When I told her no, she became even more agitated. Then I decided to go swimming and Jeni tried to stop me. "Don't go." She repeated it over and over. But I did swim. All the while Jeni tried to talk me out of the water. Eventually it got dark, she still pleaded with me, but when I looked, she was gone and in her place was an owl. When the owl warned me to get out of the water I was suddenly scared and I got out." Ice fiddled with the fraying knee of his jeans.

"Mmm. Owls symbolize the souls of the departed, they're messengers of death. Ice, I fear the owl is another bad omen."

A coldness crept into Ice's chest and spread throughout his torso. "What do you think the dream meant?"

"Only time will tell, but it's a warning for sure. Be careful." Nik studied his apprentice. "Anything else?"

Ice shook his head and started to get up, then sat back down. "Nik, she scraped her ankle in the river. If the manitou escapes, will it go after Jeni? Is she in danger?"

"At first, he'll take whoever is the easiest prey. Anyone within his reach will be in danger." Nik's brows drew together to form deep creases in his forehead. "Her blood in combination with the statue likely linked her with the creature. He'll be able to sense her power over him and will know it can be used in reverse."

"Does that mean she can help us?"

Nik shrugged. "An outsider won't understand our ways. She wouldn't believe you. Better to get the statue. We can wield it ourselves."

Ice sighed and moved to the doorway. Get the statue. Easier said than done. Yet the sooner it was out of Jeni's possession, the more likely she'd be safe. As Ice lifted the hide, the medicine man spoke again.

"Ice?"

Ice looked over his shoulder.

"Don't go swimming."

We are what we imagine.
Our very existence consists in our imagination of
ourselves...
The greatest tragedy that can befall
us is to go unimagined.

—N. Scott Momaday, *Kiowa-Cherokee*

CHAPTER 4

Jeni loitered in the kitchen drying the dinner dishes. Though she'd been told they could air-dry, this was an excuse to stand at the kitchen window looking in the direction of the resort office. Since she hadn't seen Ice yet today, she hoped he'd show up this evening, and it would be better if he didn't knock on the door—no one needed to know he was here, especially Tyler.

When she spotted Ice crossing the lawn, she threw the towel over the remaining dishes, stuffed her feet into shoes, and grabbed her jacket on the way out the door.

His face lit up when he saw her emerge from the cottage. She smiled nervously, ignoring the warm feeling in her chest. Gosh darn Carolyn! Her friend's comments about Ice this morning had her feeling self-conscious now.

"How was work?" Jeni asked.

"Enlightening."

Jeni frowned a little at Ice's response, wondering if it was supposed to be funny. She headed away from the cottage, toward the resort drive, and Ice fell into step beside her. She glanced at him, waiting for an explanation of the odd answer, but he merely shrugged and shook his head slightly.

"Let's walk over this way." Jeni pointed to the right. "I haven't seen any part of the resort past our place."

She hoped Ice didn't take her suggestion the wrong way. She wanted to stay away from the cottage and be alone with him—but not for the reason he might think. Her objective was to avoid further harassment from her cousin.

Ice was quiet and appeared contemplative—not open and talkative like last night. Jeni felt she didn't know him well enough to ask him if anything was wrong, so she decided to just get him talking. "So, you're in high school? Or are you finished?"

"Almost finished. I'm homeschooled."

"By your mom?"

"Yeah, she works days and goes over lessons with me at night when I need it. A lot of the stuff I can figure out on my own. Actually, I'm working on a Calc class now. Then I'll be completely finished with high school." He paused, as if deciding whether or not to say more, then continued. "I went to a public elementary school until it was deter...I found out that, well...I was asked to apprentice our tribe's medicine man."

Jeni glanced at him, eyes wide. "You're like a

medicine-man-in-training?"

Ice chuckled. "Sure. You could say that. Anyway, that's why I'm homeschooled. Beside all the regular stuff, I'm learning rites, rituals…and of course, legends. I actually ended up ahead of other kids in school. I'll be seventeen when I start college in the fall."

Glad that Ice perked up, Jeni thought his mention was the perfect opening to get right to the point of his visit. But when she opened her mouth, what came out was, "Is your dad the medicine man?"

Ice snorted contemptuously. "Far from it. I've never met my father."

"Oh. Sorry."

"Don't be. Nik—the medicine man—is a great role model. I'm lucky to spend so much time with him."

"What do you…*do*…in medicine man training?"

From the corner of her eye, Jeni saw Ice wore an amused expression, but he answered her question. "In the beginning it was mostly about being in tune with the world around me. Paying attention to the environment; observation. Then I learned various ceremonies—some I now know well enough to perform—although as long as Nik is medicine man, I only assist. Most recently I've been learning about medicine man tools."

They'd passed two cottages and now reached the woods that marked the edge of the resort's property. Turning toward the lake, they skirted the trees. The aroma of damp earth filled Jeni's nose—a smell she always associated with rainy days and worms.

"Tools? What kind of tools?"

Ice glanced over at her. "Uh…it would all sound crazy to you. Tell me something about you. What's it like in Detroit?"

"Wait a minute." Jeni stopped, hands on her hips. "I consider myself pretty open-minded; tell me at least one tool."

Ice surveyed her face for a moment and gave a small shrug. "Okay…we use medicine stones." He continued to stroll toward the beach.

"Like, actual stones?"

"Yeah, small rocks that help us find things or see things, like visions, dreams, premonitions." He held up his hand. "Don't ask how they work—I couldn't tell you—but they do work, I've seen it. All I know for sure is it has a lot to do with faith."

"I think it sounds pretty cool." They'd reached the sand and slowed. Jeni kicked at the ground to expose partially-hidden rocks, realizing she was looking for Petoskey stones: a product of spending a lot of time in northern Michigan. "To answer your question, I actually live north of Detroit—suburbia—where we love cars and rock-and-roll," she giggled. "And I go to regular public school. No special talents or claim to fame."

"What do you like to do?" Ice grinned. "You know, when you're not driving or listening to music."

Jeni shrugged. "I'm in Drama Club. I read a lot. I love to bake." Wow. That sounded pretty lame.

"And learn about mythology?"

She looked at Ice to see if he was making fun of her, but he appeared sincere. "Yeah, I can't help it. It fascinates me—things people have believed for centuries; stories told to teach or warn other generations. Have you seen the 'ology' books? I think Dragonology came first. Then Wizardology, Mythology, Monsterology, Vampirology...you get the idea. I have most of them." Jeni laughed. "I know: geek."

Ice smiled but didn't say anything.

Awesome. Nothing like sounding like a babbling idiot. Maybe it was time to get to the subject. "So...tell me about my statue. The underwater lynx—or what else did you say? Man..."

"Manitou. It means spirit—not in the sense of like, a ghost—he's regarded as sort of an other-than-human person."

"Like a person that takes the shape of a big cat? A shape-shifter?"

"No. He always looks like your statue—cat form, with the copper horns and scales. A lot of the myths call him a serpent. I think because in the water, with the long tail trailing behind the body, he probably does look like a giant snake."

The sun had dropped behind the trees on the horizon. There was still plenty of light out on the water, but dusk had settled around the buildings. As they passed by the cottage, Jeni noticed a few of her family members stacking wood in the firepit.

"In Ojibwe legend, Mishebeshu is the baddest of the bad; sneaky, manipulative, and unpredictable. Even grown-ups have a profound fear of him."

They'd walked the length of the resort, stopping near a picnic table, and Ice leaned against it. Jeni perched on the edge of the bench next to where Ice reclined with his arms loosely folded over his chest. He stretched out his long legs, and crossed his ankles. Jeni watched him as he talked. The blue highlights in his thick black hair shone in the waning light. Prominent cheekbones put part of his face in shadow. Her heartbeat quickened, and she dropped her gaze, concentrating on what he said.

"…they used to put tobacco in the water whenever they went swimming or wanted to cross a lake, hoping to be spared. But if Mishebeshu's mind was made up, no gift or sign of respect would change it. He might ignore you or drown you, or even steal your children."

"Dang." Jeni shivered slightly, burrowing her hands deep into her jacket pockets. Dusk had quickly turned into night. She studied the darkness surrounding them, then focused on the flickering fire three cottages away. "Want to go over by the fire?"

As they approached, she was relieved to note that Tyler wasn't part of the group. She'd thought about sitting on the deck rather than joining the small crowd, then noticed all the deck chairs encircled the fire.

"Here, you guys can have the swing." The wood swing from the yard had also been moved by the fire, and Jeni's aunt vacated it, waving her arm for them to sit. Before Jeni could object, her mom asked Ice if he wanted a hot dog.

"Yeah, that would be great. I haven't had dinner." He sat down on the swing and accepted the hot dog stick.

It all happened so fast that Jeni was flustered. Her

mom passed the hot dogs to Ice and handed Jeni the bag of buns. Jeni sat down on the swing and fiddled with the bag, regaining her composure. Wits restored, she introduced him to everyone—basically, all the women and the two small kids. Apparently the men were inside watching something on TV.

Hanging out with a bunch of women didn't seem to bother Ice at all. When the little ones became tired, yet protested loudly against bedtime, Ice asked if they wanted to hear a story.

Of course they did.

Jeni smiled at him when he finished and Ice grinned back at her. She watched him chat with her aunt—pretending she was part of their conversation—thinking about describing this to Carolyn. She could only imagine what her friend would say; that he sounded too good to be true.

And they always were. Okay, she'd only hung out with two other guys. But the same thing happened both times. She was interested, at ease, having a good time, and then the guy made some kind of physical advance, ruining everything. She claimed she just wanted to be friends, but the truth was, she didn't trust them.

Eventually, her mom and aunts said they were chilly and collected up the food. "Not too much longer," Jeni's mom warned with a backward glance before she climbed the deck stairs.

The comment made Jeni realize she and Ice were now alone, and her heart started to flutter. Not that they hadn't been alone previously, she tried to tell herself. But here they sat in the glow of a campfire, side by side, gently swinging to and fro. She was acutely aware of the space between them. Whatever she was going to say next dried up in the back of her throat.

What was her problem? Nothing was going to happen here; she was on vacation for cripe's sake. Besides, she wasn't interested in Ice—not that way.

"It's hard to believe we just met," Ice said.

"Yeah, I know," Jeni managed to choke out. Her chest felt quivery and though she knew it had nothing to do with the chilly air, she jumped up. "I think we need another log on the fire." She took her time choosing and placing a few pieces of wood, contemplating the vacant chairs. Sitting elsewhere though would look stupid—and rude. She sat back down on the swing, realizing that by stoking the fire she'd committed to staying outside for a while.

Though the swing was barely moving now, some part of it still issued a rhythmic soft creak. The only other sounds were the hiss and pop of the fire.

Jeni's attempt to think of an excuse to go inside was futile; emotion overruled reason. Was it the romantic setting? Or did Ice have some kind of medicine man juju? Because every cell in her body felt drawn to him. She wanted to slide over and snug up next to him—as if he was a magnet and she was steel.

She turned to look up into his face. He wore a weird puzzled expression. "I...uh..." he looked away and then swiveled his head back.

In the flickering firelight she could swear he was looking at her mouth and her pulse picked up. He blew out a breath then met her eyes.

Suddenly Jeni felt positive he was going to kiss her. She couldn't breathe.

"I have to ask you something."

"What?" she mumbled. If he asked if he could kiss her, she'd have to refuse—wouldn't she? They'd only just met.

Still, it was just a kiss.

Never had Jeni felt so divided. Her usual cautious, practical self battled some kind of "alter-Jeni" who was willing to take the risk.

"I…I need your statue."

Jeni stared at him dumbly for a moment. "You… what?"

"I need your statue."

"The statue?" A warm flush of anger and disbelief heated her cheeks and spread throughout her body.

"Not buy it—just borrow it. I'll return it if I can."

"What do you mean if you can?" She was a world-class idiot. She actually thought he was interested in her—wanted to kiss her? "That's why you're here?"

No answer. Which meant yes.

"Why didn't you just ask me yesterday, instead of pretending—" Jeni's voice broke and she lurched off the swing.

Ice struggled to speak.

"Don't bother!" she yelled.

She raced to the cottage door and rushed through, slamming it behind her.

"Something chasing you?" her dad asked.

"Maybe it was her boyfriend," Tyler said sarcastically. "Did he turn into a werewolf when the moon came out? Ow, ow, owooooo," he howled.

Tyler's taunts earned a hard stare from his dad. "Shut up Tyler."

Jeni glared at her cousin. "Yeah, shut up," she muttered. She couldn't deal with his behavior.

Not when she couldn't comprehend her own.

✳ ✳ ✳

Ice sat motionless, staring at his knees. How had he managed to make such a mess of things? He'd felt comfortable with Jeni and her family, too; he thought the evening had progressed smoothly.

Then he looked down into Jeni's upturned face and lost it. Despite the smoky bonfire, he could smell her; the fragrance of an apple orchard in the fall. Then his gaze fell to her glossy, ripe lips and the reasonable explanation he had in mind vanished. Instead he'd just blurted something out and completely blew it.

He'd let down Nik, the tribe…his mom. His mom. Ice groaned. That was the worst—because she would be understanding.

With a heavy sigh, Ice stood. His footsteps dragged as he headed between the cottages to the resort drive.

"Ice."

Engulfed in despair, Ice didn't register the whisper until it came the second time. He turned to see Jeni's head poked out the side door. She edged outside when she saw him stop. She took a step toward the porch rail. "I'm sorry. I overreacted." She hugged her arms around her torso. "I...I do that sometimes. I should've at least given you a chance to explain."

Ice moved closer. "Yeah...well, I didn't mean to say...ask...not like that." Jeni watched him, waiting. Ice took a deep breath. "Thing is, you're not going to like the explanation anyway."

"Well," she contemplated the toe of her shoe as she bounced it on the rail. "I can't promise I'll like it, but I'll listen." When she looked up she wore the ghost of a smile.

Ice searched her face and thought for a long moment. No more lies; time to lay the cards on the table. He wasn't hopeful for any particular outcome, only resigned to do what he felt was right. "I owe you a story about your statue don't I?"

She nodded slowly, wearing a puzzled expression.

"Let's start there then. Fire?" he asked. "It's pretty chilly over here."

"Okay."

Ice took a chair, giving Jeni the option to sit as far away as she wanted. She hesitated a second and then took the seat next to him.

He told her the story Nik had told him earlier that day, about Mishebeshu and the Illinois Waterway, except he finished it with the events of the past two days. "Then, about a hundred years later, a *priestess*..." he stopped to look at her, "...buys an artifact and falls into the water with it in her pocket. Her connection to the spirits combined with the power of the statue wakes Mishebeshu. So the local medicine man sends his apprentice to find the girl and get the statue back.

If he fails, the monster will likely escape and people will start disappearing."

Jeni narrowed her eyes at him for a moment and then laughed. "I get it. Cute. You made it sound like I was part of the story."

Ice maintained a level stare. "You are part of the story."

"Right." She chuckled.

Ice watched as she searched his face, waiting for him to break into a smile or say he was kidding. "I told you wouldn't like the explanation," he said.

"Wait." Her face was serious now. "You're telling me this is why you want my statue?"

"That's what I'm telling you."

"Ice. For starters, I am not a priestess."

"Are you sure of that?"

"Pretty darn sure. I think after fifteen years I would know, or at least, would've had some kind of clue."

"You probably have had clues, but you wouldn't have recognized them for what they were." Ice leaned forward, resting his forearms on his knees. "What you have...it's an ability; a talent. You have to train in order to fulfill your potential."

Jeni didn't say anything so Ice tried an example. "Let's say you've never been snow skiing. The first time you try, you're good at it—you discover a hidden talent for snow skiing. The more you ski, the better you get. You might have had other clues—like maybe you have great balance—you just never connected that to being a natural-born skier.

"And there's this." Ice reached over and laid his hand on top of hers. He left it there until she pulled away. She crossed her arms over her chest and glanced at him warily. "What did you see?"

At first she didn't reply. When she did, her voice was low and quiet. "Flames. Figures dancing. And I heard drums. What was it? How did you do that?"

"I don't know what it was. It comes from within you, your heritage. You see it when I touch you because I also have a link to the spirit world, but mine is more developed. With Nik—if he touches me—I'm the one who sees visions."

"This is freaking me out."

"I know. I'm sorry." Ice scrubbed his hands over his face. "Jeni, the thing is…I like you. I could've fabricated a story. I could've tried to steal the statue or something. But I felt you deserved better than that."

She was quiet for a long while after that. Ice gave her time to think. There'd be more questions.

"Okay, I could maybe swallow the priestess thing. But the monster? And how could you even know I woke it up?"

"Nik received an omen."

"Convenient."

Ice sighed and rose from the chair. "I should go." Jeni made no move to stop him. "Look, even if you think everything is bull-crap, would you consider loaning me the statue? I'll bring it back. Think about it. I'll come by tomorrow morning."

He didn't wait for an answer. When the darkness enveloped him, he looked back. Jeni hadn't moved. He watched her until she got up and went inside.

He'd rolled the dice with a clean conscience. Tomorrow he'd find out just what it got him.

*One of the things the old people taught me
about the spirits was to never have a doubt.*

—*Wallace Black Elk, Lakota*

CHAPTER 5

The cottage smelled like pancakes. Jeni wondered if anyone had thought to bring chocolate chips. Chocolate chip pancakes were her favorite, and comfort food is exactly what she needed this morning to console her confused psyche.

At first she'd fled last night because her feelings were hurt; she thought Ice was thinking about kissing her and instead he asked for the statue. The experience was like running wantonly through the grass in bare feet and then unexpectedly stepping on a bee. Inside, nursing the sting, Jeni had peeped out the window. Ice looked so forlorn sitting on the swing alone with his head down. She started feeling sorrier for him than she did for herself.

So she'd gone back and poked the hive. How stupid could she be?

Everything had gone downhill from there. She hadn't slept well; waking intermittently from dreams she couldn't remember now, although she strongly suspected they involved monsters, flames, and drums. Consequently, she overslept this morning and missed the sliver of time when Carolyn was available. Now, more than ever, Jeni needed her best friend. She had no idea what she was going to tell Ice when he showed up this morning.

She wandered into the kitchen and was startled to see Tyler setting a carton of eggs next to a large bowl. His mom was at the stove frying bacon and must've noticed Jeni's look of surprise. "Tyler promised Molly he'd make her pancakes; I figured while he was at it he might as well make pancakes for everyone."

Jeni raised her eyebrows skeptically but didn't comment. She poured a glass of juice and joined Tyler's brother Jake, Jake's wife Josie, and their daughter Molly at the table. Molly bounced in her seat. "Unca Tywer's making an'mal 'cakes."

"Sheesh, Tyler, do you have to make such a mess?" his mom said.

Jeni looked over her shoulder and saw Tyler crack an egg against the counter top. Egg whites puddled on the tile surface and also ran down the outside of the bowl. His mom sighed in exasperation. "You should have Jeni show you how to crack them. She did it one-handed and still didn't make a mess."

Jeni cringed and busily flipped through a guide book on the table, acting as though she hadn't heard the exchange. Although it was awesome to hear someone tell Tyler that she could do something better than he could, she knew there'd be repercussions if she gloated.

"Oh, I can do it one-handed," Tyler said. "Watch."

Jeni felt something on her head and before she could turn, a hand smacked down, palm flat.

Molly stared across the table, wide-eyed.

Frozen in shock, it took Jeni a few seconds to comprehend that the tickling sensation on her scalp was only Tyler's fingers trailing down her hair.

She batted at his hands. "Cut it out, jerk."

Molly burst into a fit of giggles. "Do me! Do me!"

Jeni rolled her eyes. She didn't need Tyler's shenanigans today.

Other family members ambled into the kitchen and soon the first pancakes arrived at the table: a bunny-shaped one for Molly and a car for Nat. Then Tyler brought a stack of pancakes and set them in the middle of the table before he slapped a pancake on Jeni's plate from his spatula.

Heart-shaped.

Jeni's cheeks burned. She attempted to turn it around on him. "Aww, Tyler, I didn't realize you loved me so much."

But he immediately came back with, "Yeah, I'm thoughtful—I figured you'd like a reminder of your vacation romance."

Ughhhh! Jeni gritted her teeth and hacked the pancake into pieces rendering the shape unrecognizable. Her iPod might be necessary to make it through breakfast. She changed her mind though, when a single word jumped out of a conversation between two of her aunts. Her ears perked up like a dog that just heard the word 'outside,' except the word for Jeni was 'genealogy.'

"…family trees and stuff?" Tyler's mom asked.

"I guess," Aunt Jessie responded. "I thought maybe birth records or something. But I expect at least one box has all that stuff in it. And Dad was planning a trip to Grandma Marie's for more information when he got sick."

They were referring to the boxes. Again. There'd been much discussion between Jeni's mom and her siblings about sorting the boxes they'd hurried to pack and move out of Jeni's grandpa's apartment after he died.

"Really?" Tyler's mom paused with a piece of pancake on the end of her fork. "I thought he didn't like going there; he always flew Grandma out to Michigan."

"Yeah, well, he couldn't really expect his ninety-year-old mother to go poking around in her attic. She said if he wanted the information, he could clean the attic while he was up there looking for it." Aunt Jessie chuckled.

Jeni smiled a little to herself. Anyone who'd met her great-grandma Marie knew she was a feisty, spirited old lady you couldn't help but love. She did wonder though, why her Grandpa refused to visit New Orleans. He'd traveled all over the world. Besides, he grew up there. Surely he must still have some friends or other ties in the city. In fact, they were here at the Headwaters because he'd always wanted to traverse the Mississippi from beginning to end but never got the chance.

"Oh, and get this," Aunt Jessie added, "Grandma also told him he probably wasn't going to like what he found."

"Why?" Tyler's mom looked even more amused.

"She wouldn't tell him, but now I'm dying to

know what kind of skeletons are in our family closet."

Why did they have to use the word 'skeletons'? It made Jeni think of spirits and, according to Ice, she had some kind of link to that world. She shivered involuntarily. He also said the things she saw when he touched her were related to her heritage.

Jeni frowned. So her grandpa was researching the family tree and was willing to go down to New Orleans—something he apparently never did—to find more information. And Grandma Marie alluded to some kind of family secret her son was not going to like. Was any of this related to Jeni's alleged ability? Perhaps she should call her great-grandma and ask some questions. But if her aunts didn't know, was there any chance her grandma would share the secret with her great-granddaughter?

* * *

An open calculus book and blank notebook page waited patiently beside a calculator. Ice tapped the eraser end of his pencil on the tabletop, staring at an equation. He'd gathered the necessary tools for homework but still lacked one essential element: focus. His mom wouldn't be very happy if he didn't get this assignment done, but apprehension had a way of overriding all other thoughts. Though he'd never admit it to Nik, Ice worried about what Jeni thought of him.

She'd accused him of using her to get to the statue, and Ice was ashamed to admit it was true. Well, at least that's what he'd set out to do last night. The day before he'd sincerely wanted to put her at ease as well as make sure the statue was safe. Then things became complicated as he got to know her. He respected her.

He...yeah...he liked her.

So Ice made the decision to be honest last night. He could only hope that it worked.

His gaze shifted to the clock. 8:52. How early was too early for people on vacation? Ten problems, he decided. When he had ten problems done, he'd leave for the resort.

In the middle of the third problem his cell phone rang. Ice considered ignoring it since he was finally concentrating on the work at hand. He reached for the phone to see who it was. Only a number showed on the display.

Typically, Ice disregarded any number not programmed into his phone. Whether it was his desperate need for a distraction or the lingering ominous feeling after talking to Nik yesterday, something made him press the receive button.

Hysterical gibberish responded to his greeting. Ice was able to make out his own name as well as *lake* and *dad,* so he interrupted. "Slow down, I can't understand you. Who is this?"

"Kal." A gasping breath followed.

Kal? A neighbor and childhood friend, Ice ran into him only occasionally these days.

The next stream of nearly incoherent babble included the words *fishing, monster,* and *Nik.* Ice's blood went cold and he sprang from his chair.

"Kal? Kal! Where are you right now?" Ice scrambled for his car keys. "Headwaters Center...uh-uh...

all right…yeah, go back, I'll meet you at the launch near the campground. Okay, I'm on my way."

His Jeep was in gear and rolling down the driveway as Ice buckled his seat belt. He fumbled with his phone, searching the contact list for the tribal council offices when it dawned on him that Nik wasn't there—he was at the vision quest lodge. He swore under his breath. Driving out to visit Nik wasn't an option at the moment.

With a heavy sigh, Ice tossed his phone on the passenger seat. He did his best to clear his mind, pushing everything out: Kal, the statue, Jeni. Establishing a mental link with Nik was difficult at the best of times, what made him think he could do while driving? Still, he had to try—it was his only hope to get a message to Nik.

He took a deep breath, attempting to dispel the tightness in his chest, then released his death grip on the steering wheel—one hand at a time—and flexed his fingers. Concentrating only on Nik, Ice reached out for an open line of mental communication with his mentor.

Suddenly the blare of a horn broke his concentration. Ice looked both ways frantically, trying to see what prompted the warning. He was leaving an intersection and the driver to the left on the cross street held his hands up in exasperation. A quick glance in the rear view mirror told Ice all he needed to know: he'd just run a stop sign.

There'd be no communication with Nik right now.

As apprentice, Ice served as the medicine man's

back-up. Handling this incident was his responsibility so he'd better not screw it up.

Fifteen minutes later he drove in the north entrance of Itasca State Park, and followed the main park drive to the boat launch where he spotted his friend immediately. Kal stood with his forehead pressed to the roof of a car.

Ice parked the Jeep and hopped out. "Kal? You okay?"

When his friend didn't move or respond, Ice stepped behind him and placed a firm hand on his shoulder. Kal's frame began to shake as sobs tore through his chest. Ice moved his arm to encircle his friend's shoulders as he surveyed the scene.

The lake sparkled innocently in the morning sunshine. A canoe floated idly, about ten feet from shore, with a fishing rod sticking up out of it. There was no sign of Kal's father.

An icy tension settled in Ice's chest.

When Kal's sobs subsided, Ice guided him to a parking block to sit down. He took a seat next to his friend, debating what to ask first. But Kal began to speak unprompted, delivering a somber, monotone account of his morning.

Kal's father had awakened his son before dawn to go fishing on Lake Itasca. They'd arrived at the boat launch, removed the canoe from the top of their SUV, loaded up their gear, and climbed inside. As the sun rose and they both felt more awake, Kal and his dad had started a little lighthearted banter.

Ice remained silent as Kal sunk his face into his open hands. "I said his name," he whispered hoarsely.

"Oh God," he moaned. "It was my fault."

Panic welled up from Ice's gut and he swallowed to keep it from rising to the surface. The old suspicion of not speaking the name of Mishebeshu out loud had become a sort of joke among the younger generation, particularly with the advent of Harry Potter's nemesis Voldemort—"He who must not be named." "No," Ice said quietly but firmly. "It's not your fault."

Kal turned his head toward Ice and peered out from beneath the hair draped over his face. "He was telling me how my grandpa used to bring tobacco when he went fishing and I…I said *his* name out loud. A few minutes later, my line jerked like I caught a fish. A big fish." Kal stopped and drew in a shaky breath. "We were excited. My dad got the net. He…he stood up to see into the water so he could net the fish when I got it close to the boat. All of a sudden the boat got squirrely. I saw something huge just beneath the surface. My line snapped and my dad…he…"

Ice wasn't sure if Kal would be able to finish, but he didn't need to. The end of the tale was obvious.

Kal sat up and looked across the water. "He fell in." The words issued forth with a rush of air. Then he turned and stared at Ice with dead eyes. "He fell in the lake and he never came back up."

And while I stood there I saw more than I can tell and I understood more than I saw; for I was seeing in a sacred manner the shapes of all things in the spirit, and the shape of all shapes as they must live together like one being.

—*Black Elk, Holy Man of the Oglala Sioux*

CHAPTER 6

Jeni stared out the car window chastising herself for another bad decision. She'd opted to ride with her dad and uncle to avoid questions or conversation about the previous night. But on the way to the park, they'd passed a car with its front end accordioned against a tree on the side of the road. The site started a conversation about vehicle safety standards and features that Jeni had no interest in joining or listening to.

Dodging questions would've been better than being alone with her thoughts.

Although the group hadn't left the resort until after lunch, Jeni hadn't seen any sign of Ice. He'd dumped a load of crap on her last night and then abandoned her to wallow in it. Monsters? Pah! For all of her love of mythology and legends, Jeni never believed any of it was real. If she did, she'd never sleep at night.

And if monsters weren't enough, Ice also claimed

she was a priestess. Nonsense—she was just Jeni: high school student from the Detroit suburbs. There wasn't anything remotely mysterious or different about her—or her family. The skeleton in the family closet was probably nothing more than a kid born out of wedlock. Big deal.

Jeni glowered out the window. Terrific. Now this nonsense was spoiling her vacation. How could her initial impression of Ice have been so utterly wrong? Was he actually some kind of freak that got off on making up stories and messing with people's heads?

She wanted to scream. Instead, desperate for a distraction, she snatched the park map from the seat next to her and searched for the next point of interest on the Wilderness Drive. "Why can't I find the head-waters on this map?"

Her uncle glanced over his shoulder from the passenger seat. "Look at the top of Lake Itasca."

Seriously? The Mississippi flows south across the United States—it should be at the bottom of the lake. But no, the river not only started at the top of Lake Itasca, it headed north, winding its way through other small lakes until finally beginning to journey south.

Maybe this entire area was messed up—like those 'mystery spots' advertised on billboards. Maybe something in the water made the locals a little wacko.

They pulled into a parking area and her other family members piled out of the cars and headed down the trail to an observation tower. Surrounded by idle chatter, Jeni felt acutely alone. The only saving grace was that Tyler wasn't here. He and Jake decided to check out the casino.

After the quarter-mile hike, Jeni peered up at the intimidating height of the tower. Then she directed her gaze to the switchback of stairs under the observation platform. As the group migrated toward the steps, Jeni's grandma broke from the crowd and headed for a nearby bench. Jeni joined her.

"Sitting this one out?" her grandma asked.

"I'm thinking about it. I don't really care for heights, although I always love the view."

"I'd be up there if not for my old knees. You know the trick is to not look down?"

"I know, but those steps are made of metal grate—you can see right through them." Jeni marked the progress of her mom and aunts as they worked their way to the top of the tower. A thought struck her and she suddenly felt a ray of hope. "I guess I will try it," she said.

She climbed the stairs, examining the view, careful not to look down, or to get her hopes too high. At the landing before the final flight to the top, Jeni stopped. Her hand curled around the phone in her pocket. She took a deep breath and closed her eyes.

She palmed the phone in front of her and cracked one eye open. "Yes!" she murmured, seeing she had service. Her thumbs flew over the keyboard. *Can you talk?*

Familiar voices drifted down from above and Jeni dropped the phone in her pocket as her dad passed by on his way down. She mounted the remaining steps to the top platform, her fingers crossed. What time was Carolyn done at work?

As she willed her phone to buzz, Jeni gazed out

at the park. The view was spectacular—trees blanketed the ground for miles, broken only by the dappled patchwork of lakes. Even if she didn't get to talk to Carolyn, the stunning panorama was worth the climb, reminding her that she was one small human in a vast world.

Only two family members remained on the platform when her phone finally buzzed. *Just leaving work. Give me ten minutes to get home.*

"I don't have ten minutes," Jeni mumbled to herself. Quickly, she switched from the texting screen to her favorite contacts list and pressed Carolyn's name. Typing the entire conversation would've taken too long anyway.

"Hey, what's up?" Carolyn answered in a worried voice. "Is everything okay?"

"I guess it depends how you look at it," Jeni replied, letting her wry tone speak for itself. "I've got problems."

"What kind of problems?"

Jeni spewed out the short, deranged story. "I don't know what to think Car. Part of me hopes I never see him again, and part of me hopes I do—just so I can tell him off."

"Wait, wait. Back-up. For starters, he led you on to get the statue from you?"

"Yeah, well," Jeni stammered, "maybe not. It seemed like it to me, but I could've misread his intentions—you know I'm not good in that kind of situation."

"Well either way, it's a good thing you didn't kiss him, now that you know he's a jerk and a liar."

"The thing is, I really believed he was sincere."

"So what—he's just nuts?"

"That's my current theory." Jeni uttered a humorless laugh. She paused to think for a moment, realizing her mind already seemed less muddled simply by relaying her thoughts to her friend. "The one thing I keep coming back to is that I did see something when he touched my hand."

"You said he's an apprentice medicine man. Maybe he can do that?"

"Yeah. Maybe."

"Jeni, do you realize you've been defending him this entire conversation? Either somewhere inside you believe him, or you just want to believe him."

One of Jeni's aunts approached. "We're heading down," she whispered, catching Jeni's eye to make sure she heard.

"Okay." Jeni nodded to her aunt. She had to wrap the phone call up. "I'm so confused, Car. What if he comes back? Should I let him borrow the statue?"

"After him standing you up? No way. Tell him to hit the road."

Jeni started down the steel-grated steps, one hand holding the railing in a white-knuckled grip, the other clutched tightly around her phone. She agreed with Carolyn—it's what Ice deserved after treating her this way. Except she had a better idea. "You know what? I won't let him borrow it—he can have it. I don't need any reminders of this fiasco; I'd rather just forget the whole thing."

Carolyn snickered. "Oooo. That's even better—it'll certainly let him know where you stand."

"Thanks Car. I feel better now." Jeni continued making her way down the stairs. "I should go so my dad doesn't give me a hard time for talking on the phone instead of to my relatives."

"I hear ya. Good luck. Let me know what happens."

"I will." Jeni ended the call and slipped the phone into her pocket. She felt a bit more stable once she could focus her attention on making it to the bottom without looking through the grate.

Carolyn was right—she'd been defending Ice. Why? Why couldn't she apply any of Carolyn's assumptions to the situation? The answer was obvious. Jeni was there; she looked in his eyes, read his facial expressions. He was either a fantastic actor or—

Or what?

Telling the truth?

Yes—in his mind. Jeni's intuition told her Ice wasn't lying. Even if everything he'd told her was fictitious, he absolutely believed it.

"Well, how'd you like the tower?" her grandma asked. "Was it worth the climb?"

"Yeah, it was. The view was amazing," Jeni answered. And so was the cell signal, she wanted to add.

"Good. It's good to face your fears. I'm glad you went for it."

"Me too." They walked in companionable silence for a few minutes and then Jeni added, "But if anyone suggests caves, I'm out."

THUNDERSTONE

✳ ✳ ✳

Ice watched the medicine man devour half of his sandwich, amazed that Nik showered and donned a fresh flannel shirt and jeans before eating. "Between you and me," Nik said, "I hate fasting. Always have."

Ice allowed a small smile. Any reminder that his teacher had downfalls and weaknesses like everyone else helped quell the overwhelming thought of filling Nik's shoes one day. Since he'd relayed Kal's account of his father's disappearance on the drive back from the vision quest lodge, Ice waited patiently while his mentor chewed.

When a quarter of his sandwich remained, Nik finally spoke up. "During my quest, I sought my ancestors for advice but it seemed they were elsewhere. If the monster is already free, I understand why." He leaned back in his chair and gazed past Ice, recalling his vision. "At first, I followed the sound of thunder into a forest of unearthly quiet. No animals rustled in the undergrowth; no birds called from the branches above. Not even an insect buzzed in my ear." He crunched a few chips then continued. "I left the woods in pursuit of the storm and came upon an old ground-level well with a shattered top. Shards of wood littered the ground as if the cover had exploded outward." He met Ice's gaze. "No mystery there, considering what we know now."

Ice nodded. "Escape." Muted shouts followed by laughter filled the short silence. Seconds later, the clatter of bikes and skateboards on cement came from the sidewalk in front of Nik's house. The carefree sounds suddenly made Ice long for those days of blissful innocence.

"As I crossed a field I came upon the dismembered bodies of two Thunderbirds, turkey vultures..." Nik trailed off. He looked at his sandwich, but didn't pick it up.

Ice draw in a sharp breath. Vultures? That couldn't be good.

Nik resumed. "The storm seemed to stall over a lake. I finally spotted a living creature—a Thunderbird circling beneath the clouds. I couldn't make out what kind of bird it was. At first I thought it was a hawk—since a hawk brought the omen—then I realized the form appeared more bulky or compact. Perhaps an owl. Lightning struck over the water and then over the beach. After the second flash, the bird had disappeared." He sighed. "I hope these signs and messages become clear to us soon so we can make use of the knowledge. I would've liked more direct spiritual guidance."

Nik finished his sandwich while Ice pondered the vision; the ice cubes in his water glass tinkling as he absently rocked it back and forth. "What do turkey vultures symbolize?"

"Generally, the balance of life and death. They feed on carrion—dead animals. They use death to promote life," Nik replied.

"Yeah, I figured it was something like that. You said there were two of them. Do you think...maybe they represented the guardians? You know, of the manitou. They used their own death to keep us safe, right?"

Nik's eyebrows flicked upward as he considered Ice's explanation. "It makes sense," he said, nodding. "In order to escape, the manitou needed to get past the guardians. But who or what destroyed them?" Then the older man's thoughtful expression unexpectedly transformed into a smile. "You're really starting to think like a medicine man, Ice."

A little embarrassed by the compliment, yet immensely pleased, Ice didn't comment.

"We need to investigate, see if we can find some clues how the manitou escaped. Did you get the statue from the girl?"

Ice froze and then dropped his head on his open palms. "Uhh," he groaned. "I was supposed to see her this morning. Then Kal called. All I could think was that I needed to talk to you. Then the debate with the council about reporting the death to the authorities went on forever. I completely forgot."

"Then you need to go get it. I'll go to the lake and examine the area where the underwater lynx was imprisoned."

"I'll go with you. It's on the way," Ice offered.

"No, it's imperative that you get the statue. I'm just going to poke around the shore—I'll stay well away from the water."

Ice checked the clock on Nik's microwave. The resort was a good half hour away and he hadn't had a chance to shower yet today. He should get going if he wanted to see Jeni today. He got up and took his glass to the sink, breathing deeply to alleviate the tightness in his chest. He wondered if Jeni would be angry. She had every right to be.

As usual, the medicine man sensed Ice's tension. "I know it may not be easy getting the statue, but we must get the monster under control before he takes another victim."

Ice met his mentor's gaze and nodded as he let out a shaky laugh. "Yeah, no pressure."

✹ ✹ ✹

Jeni's heart lurched when she saw the wash of headlights on the cabin next door. She shook her head; mentally admonishing herself for still thinking Ice would show up. A glance to her right, where her mom was washing a pan, confirmed that the dishes were almost done. Thank goodness. She could get away from the window and distract herself with TV or a book.

A car door slammed confirming someone had arrived at this cottage or the one next door. Then a second door slammed. Most likely Tyler and Jake, back from the casino. Jeni frowned at the twinge of disappointment she felt. Did she not have any control over her own emotions? Why should she care if Ice showed up or not?

She shouldn't.

Except she did. Because she had questions. Questions that would haunt her perpetually if left unanswered. Like how come Ice acted as if the "situation" was dire last night and then completely blew it off today?

Though she had no way of knowing it, some

answers had just walked through the door.

"Daddy!" Molly scampered into the room and threw herself at Jake.

"Hey," Jeni's mom said. "I hope you won big because you missed dinner."

"I always win big." Tyler grinned and sauntered into the living room.

Jake rolled his eyes. "I guess it depends on your definition of big." He laughed.

Jeni finished rinsing the last pan and balanced it carefully on the stack of clean dishes in the dish drainer. She could hear Tyler launch into a story in the other room as she dried her hands. On her way to the bedrooms at the back of the cottage Jake stopped her.

"Jeni."

"Yeah?" She looked over her shoulder.

"You might want to hear this." He jerked his thumb in the direction of the living room.

"Really?" Jeni had no reason to think Jake might be playing some kind of trick on her, so when he nodded, she stepped into the living room doorway.

"…was pretty wasted and talking way louder than he thought. His buddy kept trying to hush him up, which of course made everyone at the table want to hear the story." Tyler scanned his audience, reveling in the attention. "So it sounded like what happened is a father and son went fishing this morning on Lake Itasca. The son hooked a fish and when his dad tried to net it, he fell out of the boat. The son never saw him again."

Tyler paused for effect, assuring all eyes were on him. "But he did see something in the water.

Something big—way bigger than the canoe they were in."

"What kind of something?" someone asked.

Blood rushed in Jeni's ears, obliterating whatever answer Tyler gave. She stood stock still as dread spread throughout her abdomen and formed a heavy mass.

"…Ice?"

The name permeated her numb brain bringing her back to the conversation.

"He was first on the scene," Tyler said. "I guess the guy was his friend or something."

Jeni backed from the doorway and slipped down the hall to the bathroom. She shut the door behind her, locked it, then just stood there for a moment, eyes closed, hands pressed to her chest. Her heart beat at a marathon pace. What if it was true? Oh God, what if everything Ice told her was true?

She'd been feeling sorry for herself all day when a man had actually died. She should've given Ice the statue yesterday. If he could've stopped this—that man's blood was on her hands! It was her fault for being stubborn and selfish.

Having trouble forcing air into her lungs, Jeni leaned over the sink and splashed water on her face, causing her to draw in a sharp breath. Then she let the cold water run over her wrists. Her head began to clear and she breathed deeply. "Overreact much?" she asked her reflection and then uttered a weak laugh.

She went over the story in her mind again, trying to see all the angles. Just because Ice was mentioned didn't necessarily mean this had anything to do with her. The guy simply called Ice because he was his friend. Maybe the man hit his head on the boat or had a heart attack—there could be many reasons he didn't rise to the surface—it didn't mean a monster got him. And who knows what the guy thought he saw in the water? With the amount of trees surrounding Lake Itasca, dead wood and rotting logs must be plentiful in the lake.

No wonder Ice didn't show up if this happened just this morning. A fragment of guilt crept into Jeni's chest to mingle with the waning panic. She'd been so angry, but maybe Ice still planned to come.

She took a deep breath and released it slowly. Okay. She was okay. She should be able to face the family. Once she was settled in front of the TV or possibly playing cards, the fear burning in the pit of her stomach would fade.

She was wrong about that.

Knowledge can be learned but until it is truly experienced, it does not become wisdom.

—Selo Black Crow, Lakota

CHAPTER 7

Knowing it was rather late, Ice hesitated before knocking on the door outside the dark kitchen. It seemed all the events of the day conspired to keep him from getting here. What would the new roadblock be? Peering around the edge of the cottage he could see lights from the living room spilling through the sliding glass door. Back at the side door, he held his breath and knocked.

Moments later the kitchen flooded with light and Jeni's dad approached the door.

"Great," Ice mumbled under his breath.

"Jeni," her dad called as he turned the knob. He didn't sound too pleased. But he held the door open so Ice could come inside. "Little late don't you think?"

"Yeah, sorry about that, sir. There's been a lot going on."

"Jeni'll be out in a minute."

The aroma of popcorn hung in the air. Ice fidgeted with the zipper on his hoodie, praying no one else came in the room. As soon as Jeni entered he spoke. "I'm sorry I didn't come this morning," he stammered. "My friend—"

"It's okay," Jeni cut him off with a wave. Her brow furrowed but her eyes were unreadable. "I heard about the…the accident." She gestured to the table. "Do you want to sit down…something to drink?"

He was about to decline then realized all the moisture had left his mouth as soon as Jeni entered the room. "Water?" The table had long benches instead of chairs and Ice sat down, his back to the table. "It was my friend, Kal's, dad. Drowned, we assume. The body's still missing. Kal's really busted up about it." Ice leaned forward, forearms on knees.

Jeni pulled a bottle of water from the refrigerator and handed it to him as she joined him on the bench. He heard her draw in a breath as if to say something and then stopped. He expected her to have questions so he took a long drink of water, giving her plenty of time to get her thoughts together. Finally she spoke. "What happened?"

"What did you hear?"

"They were fishing on Lake Itasca. His dad fell in and never came up—" Jeni examined her nails for a long moment while a commercial droned in the other room. "The son—your friend—said he saw something in the water. Is that what he told you?" She turned and met his eyes.

Ice nodded then went back to studying the floor. He'd resolved to tell her only what she wanted to know.

Then she asked. "What…what did he see?"

"Something huge. Snakelike."

He watched her reaction. Her eyes widened and

she looked away, but not before Ice saw the raw fear within. "You think…" she stammered.

He didn't make her say it. "No, we don't *think.* We have no doubt. That wasn't the only accident today." Ice waited for her to look at him. "I was on my way over here and Nik went looking for the cave, you know, the prison. He was attacked."

"Attacked? Is he okay?"

"He was hit on the head from behind." Ice felt his throat closing up and forced himself to swallow before he continued. "He's in the hospital in Bemidji. I don't know what'll happen…he's old…"

He took a deep breath and curled his fingers around the stone in his pocket. *Here goes nothing.* "When the bank loans someone money, they expect that person to have collateral—things with enough value to cover the loan, right?"

Jeni drew back in surprise and looked sideways at him. "What are you talking about?"

"Collateral." Ice withdrew a blue stone and held it out on his palm. "It's not shaped like anything, but it is a real medicine stone like I told you about. This one's a dream stone. I'll leave this if you'll let me take your statue. As collateral." He allowed a tiny smile.

"Dream stone."

Ice wasn't sure if it was a question, but he answered it anyway. "Yeah. For premonitions…like an answer to a question. Or sometimes they're warnings."

Jeni wore a faraway look, he wasn't sure she'd heard anything he just said. "Wow…uh…wait." Jeni popped up from the bench and left the room. She returned a minute later with her statue. She held it out to Ice. "I don't know what's out there, but if you think this will help, take it. You don't have to give me any... collateral."

"I'd feel better about it." She shook her head and leaned against the counter, facing him.

Green. He realized her eyes were green.

Ice rose from the bench. "Thanks, I'll return it. If I can."

"If you can? You said that last time. What's that supposed to mean?"

Ice shrugged. "What we're attempting to do is dangerous. Nik was hurt just investigating." Man, that sounded so grave—which it was, but he wasn't here to lay a guilt trip on Jeni. "You didn't think battling a mythological monster would be a walk in the park did you?" He gave her a full-blown smile.

It had the desired effect. Jeni returned the smile and the cloud of tension surrounding them dispersed. "Well, from what I've read—and I've read a lot—those battles are never easy," Jeni said. "But heroes usually have a special weapon. I guess I just gave you yours."

He looked down into her upturned face and flashed back to the night at the campfire. The urge to kiss her was overwhelming. No, that's not why he was here. His business was done—he should go.

But the seriousness and the potential hazards of what needed to be done made him feel rather reckless. If Nik wasn't okay, Ice was going after the monster alone. So he took a step closer, crossing the line between safe distance and personal space. Jeni didn't move.

"Mmm, hero? I don't know about that." He

inched a little closer—close enough to feel her radiant body heat. "But I am going into battle…" Ice wondered if Jeni could hear his heart pounding. He made an attempt at a calming breath. "In case I don't make it…I thought…" he was going to ask to kiss her, but when she raised her chin and stretched toward him, the unspoken question was answered.

His lips touched hers and—

She jerked her head back, a shocked look on her face.

Ice backed away and suddenly it dawned on him. "Vision?"

Jeni nodded.

"Well, that's a problem."

"Ya think?" She laughed a little, but Ice thought he detected restrained disappointment. Without thinking, he opened his arms. She contemplated him for a second and then stepped forward. Her hair smelled like pears. He squeezed her gently, relishing her warm softness, then turned and slipped out the door.

He'd reached the grass when he heard her call out. "Ice." He turned.

"Be careful."

* * *

Jeni watched Ice disappear into the darkness, a tumult of emotions churning inside her. His intrinsic sincerity made her want to believe him. The rational side of her still insisted all that was out there was a submerged tree or an unnaturally large fish.

Alter-Jeni—who was becoming more and more bold lately—thought maybe she needed to open her mind to other possibilities.

The blue stone lay on the table. Jeni wasn't sure when he put it there; she hadn't intended to take it. Whether or not she got the statue back didn't seem very important anymore. She picked up the stone and headed for the bedroom. With her grandma fast asleep, it was the next best thing to being alone. And she had a lot to think about.

When her dad told her Ice was here to see her, she'd run to the bedroom and exchanged her pajama pants for a pair of jeans. Then she grabbed a hoodie and pulled it on over her cami. In a hurry and distracted, the night-light had been sufficient. Now she felt the need to dispel the lurking shadows, so Jeni turned on her book light and propped it up on the nightstand.

Once she was back in her pajamas, she slipped beneath the covers and settled on her side. She plucked the blue stone off the nightstand and set it next to her pillow. Though she stared at the stone, the kiss hovered foremost in her thoughts. Well, the almost-kiss. How did that happen? Who was she? For that matter, who was he? She barely knew him and he'd told her this cockamamie story, yet came across so real—so genuine.

Her physical reaction to him was unprecedented. Apparently she'd just experienced the definition of chemistry, because the closer he got, the closer she wanted him to come. And then, when she was sure he intended kiss her, she didn't turn away, she leaned in.

Chemistry. Perhaps the missing link in her

other relationships. (If she could even call them relationships.)

Suddenly she huffed an ironic chuckle. Awesome. The first guy Jeni actually wanted to touch her—couldn't touch her. At least not without making her see visions.

Figured.

Wow. She had so much to tell Carolyn.

Jeni trailed her fingers across the stone. Emotionally drained, her eyes drifted shut.

She stood at the top of an embankment overlooking a lake. Although thick clouds blotted out any chance of moonlight, distant lightning outlined the figures of Ice and an older man working their way along the shoreline. She'd never met him, yet Jeni was certain the older man was Nik.

As they drew closer, Jeni could make out Ice's anxious face. "Will we have any influence without the statue?"

The medicine man carried some sort of pouch or bag and wore a worried frown. He patted the bag. "Medicine men have other tools." His tone sounded as though he was trying to convince himself.

They stopped at the base of the bank. Nik rummaged in the bag, removing items. He gave Ice a pack of cigarettes. "Open them," he instructed, placing the other items in easy reach.

"Give me five or six." Nik tore the filters off and emptied the tobacco on the sand in a trail from the water to the embankment. He disappeared for a minute and Jeni dropped to hands and knees at the top of the mound to peer over the edge.

Barbara Pietron

A flash of lightning showed a rough opening in the bank amidst rocks, sand, brush, and…wire? Distracted, she traced the wires and realized they ran up, over the outcropping and into the woods. Before she could investigate, Ice's voice drew her attention.

"Will this draw the manitou—" A rumble of thunder drowned out the rest.

"—ncestors used tobacco to mollify him or show respect, so it should at least get his attention," Nik answered. "His motivation, however, is hunger. And greed."

Nik and Ice climbed the bank and laid flat in the brush, peering through the foliage. The forest behind them moved in the wind of the coming storm. Nik nudged Ice and they studied the lake intently. Jeni gazed across the water and saw two sharp points pierce the surface of the lake. They drifted toward shore, followed by a large snake-like object.

Jeni's eyes grew wide as the enormous head protruded from the water. Cunning, elliptically-shaped eyes scanned the shoreline. Black liquid streamed off the creature's scales as it extracted itself from the lake.

It was her statue come to life.

The dragon-like monster maneuvered its considerable bulk across the strip of sand to the opening in the bank. As soon as its head was inside, Nik and Ice silently descended the slope. They perched on either side of the hole marking the beast's progress.

The medicine man raised something in his fist and looked to the sky, his lips moving noiselessly. Soon, only the creature's massive tail remained visible.

Without warning, the monster's tail lashed to

the left, slamming Ice hard against the rocks. His unconscious body slumped to the ground. Jeni winced and cried out, though she made no audible sound. In a fluid motion, the tail swung back to the right and caught Nik under the arms. It lifted him from the ground and flung him out into the water.

Terrible laughter resonated. "You have no power over me." The voice came from everywhere—penetrating her skull and sending an icy shiver down her spine.

The beast disappeared. Poised to jump, Jeni jerked backward, realizing the creature had turned around. The snout emerged from the cave opening and its mighty jaws clamped over Ice's limp form. Screaming soundlessly, Jeni scrambled to the shoreline. She grabbed for Ice's arm, her ghostly fingers passing right through.

The underwater manitou plunged into the water, sinking beneath the surface.

Horrified, Jeni gaped at the swirling water and Nik's figure bobbing facedown nearby. Suddenly the bestial tail spiraled up out of the water and smacked down over Nik's body, curling around him and taking him to the depths as well.

Jeni let out a silent wail of despair.

She clawed up the bank and ran blindly into the woods with no idea where she was or where she was going. Sobs wracked her body and tears blurred her vision. Her toes struck an overgrown log and she stumbled, somehow managing to stay on her feet, but the ground was a minefield of them and the next time she tripped, she went down.

She opened her eyes and stared at her book light. She didn't move for a long moment, slowly comprehending where she was and what had happened.

She'd fallen asleep with the book light still on... and dreamed.

Her hand drifted up to feel her cheek, still damp with tears. The dream was so vivid, so real, Jeni expected to find leaves in her hair when she sat up. Slipping out of bed, she crept to the bathroom for a tissue. She dried her eyes and blew her nose. As she climbed back into bed, she realized the blue stone no longer sat next to her pillow.

As she searched the area with her small light, she remembered Ice had called it a dream stone; perhaps it was the reason for the realistic dream. When she didn't find the stone in the bed, Jeni guessed it had fallen on the floor. She'd have to find it tomorrow. There was no way she was going to search under the bed in the dark.

Feeling spooked, Jeni grabbed a magazine. She tried to tell herself that after the day she had, the content of the dream wasn't hard to justify. Reasoning didn't help. Neither did *Seventeen.* Anxiety gnawed at her. What else did Ice say about the stone?

Premonitions and...Jeni's heart skipped a beat... warnings.

What if the events she saw were destined to happen? She must tell Ice.

Maybe he'd say that's not what the stone did. Maybe a medicine stone had no effect on her. Even as she tried to form plausible responses, they were buried by her intuition.

What bothered Jeni more than anything else were the words: you have no power over me. If the medicine man had no power over the creature, who did?

Her head immediately rejected her first thought. But Jeni felt it lingering in her heart.

What works for us is who we are.
It is empowering.
We know our blood, we know our heritage.

—Carol J. Jorgensen, Tlingit

CHAPTER 8

Jeni hadn't slept much, though that's not the reason she was agitated. She needed to talk to Ice and had no way to contact him. Her mom, grandma, and aunts went to some kind of market. Her dad was fishing, and Jake and Josie took Molly somewhere. Unfortunately that left Tyler, Nat, and Nat's dad at the cottage with Jeni.

She wandered around the resort, hoping she might run into Ice, and wishing her friend wasn't at work. Carolyn hadn't been the first thing on her mind this morning and now it was too late to contact her.

A thorough search of her bed and the floor around it had produced nothing. The blue stone seemed to have vanished. The ominous connotations of the missing stone on top of the contents of the dream itself filled her with a sense of urgency that grew as time went on. By lunchtime, desperation overwhelmed her. With no other prospects, Jeni swallowed her pride and entered the resort office.

"Ice?" The woman peered at Jeni over the top of

the glasses perched on the end of her nose. "Yeah, I know who you mean—with the blue eyes. Haven't had him do anything here since last summer."

"Oh...I..." Jeni struggled to recover from the unexpected information. "Well he was here the other day. Do...do you have a number for him? He left something behind...at our cottage, I mean."

The woman appraised Jeni, hands on hips. "I don't mean to be rude honey, you seem like a nice girl and all, but you understand I can't do that, don't you?"

"Yeah, I guess." Jeni took a step back. "Thanks," she mumbled. Her head snapped up. "Maybe you could call him? Tell him he left a...a tool at our place?" The flimsy explanation sounded so contrived, she felt her cheeks burn.

"A tool? If Bernie's hiring help without telling me, he's in big trouble." She pushed her glasses up and began scanning pages in a weekly calendar. "If I talk to Ice, honey, I'll let him know about the tool."

"Thank you." If Ice did get the call, he'd definitely wonder what was up.

On her way back to the cottage she remembered Ice said Nik was in the hospital. In Bemidji. By the time she came through the side door, Jeni decided it was worth a try. What she saw in her dream could happen tonight—she had to try to contact somebody. Problem was, with only a learner's permit, she either needed an adult in the car or someone to drive her there. Nat's dad was out of the question.

Which left Tyler.

Jeni opened the refrigerator. The best way to get

a guy to do something is bribe him with food. Good grief, she must be some kind of crazy to even consider doing this.

Aside from the phenomenal sandwich she made for Tyler, Jeni thought he was persuaded by sheer boredom. He downshifted and accelerated on the blacktop. "You know where we're going, right?" he asked.

"Yeah, Ice said Bemidji. I figured I'd try to look it up on my phone if we happened to get service along the way, but I did bring a map," Jeni said, extracting it from her purse and holding it up.

"I can't believe you talked me into this," he grumbled. "I hate hospitals."

"I told you, you don't have to come in." In fact, she was counting on him not going in with her. "And you might not have to wait; Ice might be able to drive me back." She had to make him think this was prearranged; that Ice would be there.

"I'm not so sure your parents would be thrilled if I came back without you." Tyler looked over at her. "Why is it so important that you go to the hospital to see this guy—Nik? You don't even know him."

"I know…it…it's important to Ice, though." She'd given this story some thought ahead of time.

"Right. And…" Tyler waved his hand to indicate she should continue. "You said you'd explain on the way," he reminded her.

"You know that statue I picked up the first day?" Jeni explained that Ice was apprenticed to Nik. She wanted to stick as close to the truth as possible without telling Tyler everything. How could she? Look how she'd reacted—he'd laugh her right out of the car. "Ice borrowed it so Nik could see it. And it turns out that he wants to use it for some tribal ceremony, but he has to ask my permission first since I own it."

"You couldn't tell him it was okay over the phone?"

"No. It's a cultural thing. He has to ask me in person."

"The dude's in the hospital but he's still going to do this ceremony?"

"I guess so." Jeni fell silent. She saw no reason to embellish her lies and dig a deeper hole than she'd be able to crawl out of, should it come to that. She checked the map. "Take a left at the light."

Tyler slid a disc into the stereo and Jeni breathed a silent sigh of relief. She'd been through the dream over and over and kept coming back to the same answer: *she'd* woken the monster; therefore *she* had to put it back to sleep. It's the only thing that made sense.

A man had lost his life—his blood was technically on her hands—she couldn't step back and let it happen again. Nor could she allow Nik and Ice to put themselves in harm's way to correct a problem that she'd caused. Especially after she saw what would—or could—happen to them.

"Turn right up here. I think we'll see it after that."

Tyler pulled up in front of the hospital's main entrance. "This won't take long right?"

"Right."

The antiseptic smell that barraged Jeni as she pushed the door open raised an immediate lump in her throat. How many times had she gone to the hospital to see her grandpa before he died? Each time he looked less like the man who'd read her stories on his lap and taught her how to win at checkers.

She swallowed and approached the reception desk. Because of her recent experience, Jeni had already thought about how to find someone in the hospital when she only knew his first name. She hoped her story worked. "Hi. My boyfriend is here seeing his grandpa, he asked me to meet him here."

"What's the patient's name?"

"Nik…oh gosh, I don't know his last name."

"What's your boyfriend's last name?"

"Oh…uh…no," Jeni shook her head. "It's his mom's dad."

"Mmm. Is he a Nicholas?"

"I'm not sure, sorry."

The woman stared at her for a moment. "All right. You wouldn't happen to know why he's here? That might help narrow it down."

"A head injury. He had some kind of accident."

"Now we're getting somewhere. That rules out quite a few areas." The woman tapped her keyboard repeatedly. "Okay, I do have a Nik, spelled N-I- K. He's in room 208. If that's not right, you just might have to wait for your boyfriend to come and get you from the lobby."

"Thanks for your help."

"Yep. Have a good one." She pointed over her left shoulder. "Those elevators."

Jeni hurried to the elevators and stepped out on the second floor. She took a deep breath as she approached room 208. She'd never met Nik, how would she know if he was the right guy or not?

Voices murmured inside the room. Jeni paused for a moment to listen. Definitely men. She peeped around the corner.

The man in the bed had a lined bronze face. A braid held his gray hair behind his head. Convinced she had the right man, any lingering doubt vanished when she saw the blue stone on the night stand by his bed. She stepped into the doorway and knocked lightly on the open door.

The man looked over in surprise. Before he could say anything, Ice's head poked around the corner. "Jeni? Wh…How…?"

"Ice. I'm glad you're here. I'm sorry to intrude, but I think I have something important you need to know."

Ice frowned. "About what?"

Jeni's gaze darted from Ice to Nik and back to Ice. "I had a dream."

Ice took her arm and drew her into the room. Nik was shaking his head. The medicine man did not look pleased. Ice gestured to the chair. The combination of nerves, the stifling warmth of the room, and the smell of bodies, medicine, and plastic made Jeni slightly nauseated. She shrugged out of her jacket before perching on the edge of the seat.

"Did you have the dream stone with you when you had the dream?" Ice asked.

Jeni nodded. "I was looking at it. I fell asleep." She saw the men exchange glances. "How did it get here? I looked everywhere for it this morning."

"When it's used, it returns to the medicine man

who found it."

Nik gave Ice a look that Jeni couldn't discern and cleared his throat. "What did you see?"

She told them everything she could remember. She locked eyes with Ice. "It was a premonition, wasn't it?" He nodded but Nik spoke.

"It wasn't your place to use the stone."

Jeni felt her cheeks flush. "I…I didn't mean to."

"A dream stone shows a possible reality; something that could happen if circumstances don't change."

She summoned her courage and looked directly at Nik. "Let me help. If I join you…it changes things. The dream can't come true."

"Absolutely not."

Jeni turned to Ice but he shook his head. "It's too dangerous."

She swiveled her head from one face to the other. "But you have no power over the monster—that's what it said. *I* woke it up; apparently I do have some kind of influence. It's my fault your friend's dad is dead." She choked a little as her emotions boiled up. "I should make it right."

"Calm down." Nik said. "In your dream, did I have the statue?"

"No." Her answer was clipped. She'd gone to a lot of trouble to get here, to tell them this, to offer to help, and she was being treated like a naughty child!

"There you go. I have it now—thanks to you." Nik's smile, topped by an annoyed stare, only made things worse. "We can handle things from here."

Jeni didn't know what to say. She glared at Ice,

though she didn't know what she expected him to do—stick up for her maybe? "Fine," she said through clenched teeth. She whipped her jacket from her lap as she got up. It skimmed the top of the nightstand and sent objects skittering. Jeni grabbed the little plastic pitcher of water before it went over and shoved it back from the edge. Then without further comment or a good-bye, she stalked from the room.

And ran into Tyler. Literally. Standing with his arms crossed and a glower on his face, he blocked her path to the elevator. "Just what the hell are you up to?"

"None of your business." She dodged around him, not sure if she wanted to scream or cry—or throw up.

Tyler didn't say anything as they waited for the elevator across from the nurse's station, but she could feel the anger emanating from him. How long had he been standing in the hallway? How much had he heard? Jeni prayed they wouldn't be in the elevator alone.

They weren't. Ice slid through the doors just before they closed.

The silence was palpable. Ice stole sideways glances at Jeni, who stood staring straight ahead with her hands stuffed into her jean's pockets. Tyler leaned against a sidewall, scowling at the two of them.

"I can drive Jeni back," Ice offered.

"No." Tyler was adamant. His fury unnerved Jeni. Their rules of engagement had never encompassed anything beyond rivalry.

Once outside, Jeni stopped on the sidewalk.

"Tyler, I…I need to talk to Ice."

He spun around so fast, Jeni recoiled. His eyes were full of indignation.

"Please?" she added in a small voice.

"Three minutes," he said, checking his watch. "Talk fast."

Jeni took Ice's arm and pulled him away. "I know I shouldn't have shown up unannounced. It's just…I was worried. I thought what I saw might happen—tonight even. I decided I wanted to help and I thought Nik would be happy…" she paused for a breath. "Ice, do you believe the statue is all you need?"

"Nik said we can do it by ourselves. It's better this way—I don't want to put you in danger."

Jeni's face flushed as resentment surged through her. "The way I understand it, I'm the one who put people in danger."

"Jeni, you can't blame yourself—you had no idea. Besides, we're equipped to handle this."

"Are you?" She shot back. "Is that why Nik's in the hospital?"

"He was caught by surprise."

"Mmph. You never answered me—about the statue."

Ice didn't say anything.

"You don't agree."

"Jeni, Nik is my elder and my teacher; I'll do what he says."

"And I'm supposed to just let you and Nik go after this…this…creature or whatever it is, and put yourselves in harm's way when all this is my fault!" Tears welled in Jeni's eyes. She angrily blinked them away.

Ice grabbed her by the arms and she looked up into his face filled with hurt and frustration. Out of the corner of her eye she saw Tyler take a step toward them.

Ice spoke calmly and quietly. "I told you the truth because I respected you. Maybe that was a mistake, but it's done. You gave me your statue and I'm grateful, but you need to let this go. Please Jeni, for my sake..." he dropped his hands to his sides.

His eyes pleaded with her.

"Okay," she mumbled. "Fine." She tore her eyes from his and quickly walked toward Tyler.

He fell into step beside her. "What. The hell. Is going on?"

Jeni knew she owed him an explanation. She dabbed the corners of her eyes with her sleeves.

Tyler's silence emphasized his expectation of an answer. When they reached the car, he didn't even put his key in the ignition.

Jeni sank into the passenger seat. Her conflicted emotions barely allowed her to think coherently. She couldn't possibly weave some grand tale on the spot.

So she told him the truth.

✸ ✸ ✸

Ice didn't return to the hospital until it was nearly dark outside. He'd spent the remainder of the afternoon venting his frustration by doing chores at home. Nik thought Ice had really screwed up by telling Jeni the truth. Heck, Ice questioned his own judgment at this point. But he knew in his heart that even if he could go back and start over, he couldn't deceive Jeni—withhold some information, maybe—but not lie to her outright.

After replaying the scene at the hospital in his head a dozen times, Ice finally called his mom. Getting his thoughts into words and out of his head helped a lot. His mom was always straightforward with him—even when the truth hurt. This time her comments confirmed what Ice already knew and hadn't yet acknowledged.

He pulled his Jeep into the hospital parking deck. He sat for a moment before getting out, resigned to trust in Nik's wisdom. He did believe that since Jeni woke the spirit while in possession of the stone figure, she should be able to control it. But if Nik could do the same thing, the medicine man's experience made him the better person for the job.

Bottom line: it didn't matter what Ice thought. He wasn't making the calls.

He just hoped he could convince Jeni to talk to him again. He couldn't help but admire her persistence and courage—she'd tracked them down to warn them and to offer her help. Which meant she believed him.

With a heavy sigh he got out of the car and headed for the hospital. As he passed the spot where they'd spoken earlier under Tyler's hawk-like stare, Ice flashed back to how stunning she'd looked—spots of scarlet high on her cheeks, her green eyes glittering with unshed tears. Her passion evidenced how much she cared which is what affected Ice the most. He'd wanted to take her in his arms but fought down the urge and walked away.

Nik was sitting up in bed, the TV on with no sound. When he saw Ice, he lifted the remote and switched it off. He waved his apprentice to the chair.

"The girl seemed angry," Nik commented.

"Seemed?"

The corners of his mouth twitched and Nik studied Ice for a long moment. "You care for this girl."

"Can we call her Jeni, please?" Ice leaned his head back on the chair and looked at the ceiling. "Yeah, I like her. More than I should for the amount of time I've known her."

He raised his head and stared at the blackness beyond the window. "I feel like I could talk to her about anything. She's different—smart—not shallow, like so many other girls I've known. And she seemed genuinely interested in me. In who I am." He dug his fingers into his hair, pressing his palms to his forehead. "And I went and messed it up."

"Give it some time. The heat of the moment will have cooled by morning." Nik leaned forward and touched Ice's hand. "If she likes you half as much as you like her, she'll get over it."

Ice closed his eyes, anticipating the imagery evoked by the medicine man's touch.

Nik squeezed and then let go.

Ice opened his eyes. Nik's contact had just provided him with the perfect opportunity to broach an embarrassing subject. He drew in a deep breath and forged ahead. "I've wanted to ask you about something…"

Nik raised his eyebrows.

"When you touch my hand like that—I see visions."

Nik nodded and settled into his pillows.

Ice swallowed, almost chickening out, but he needed answers and Nik was the only person he knew who could help him. "If I touch Jeni's hand, she sees the visions."

"Because your abilities are stronger; more developed."

Ice looked away, scanning the room. "That's not really the question." He swiped a hand through his hair. "I…I tried to kiss her and…it wasn't a good thing."

"Mmmm…that's not a common problem. Medicine women are rare in our people and it's even rarer that a medicine man and a medicine woman want to be together." He chuckled. "Too much competition."

"So there's nothing I can do?"

"Oh, I didn't say that."

He had Ice's full attention.

Nik gazed up at the ceiling for a moment, gathering his thoughts. "Everything in our lives requires balance of our three parts—free soul, ego soul, and body."

Ice nodded.

"It's your free soul which travels in dream and vision…"

Ice opened his mouth but Nik held up his hand like a policeman stopping traffic. "Wait, I'm thinking this through out loud." He returned to his discourse, "The free soul is also instinct and sensation. Your ego soul provides knowledge and reasoning."

This time when Nik paused, Ice pressed his lips together, waiting.

"When you're balanced, your ego soul allows visions to happen in its quest for knowledge. However, if your free soul dominated, it would likely abandon the visions in favor of baser instincts."

Nik looked at Ice as if he expected some reaction, but Ice wasn't quite sure where Nik was going. "So…"

Nik lifted his hands off the bed, palms up. "One of the animal kingdom's basest of instincts is to mate."

Heat bloomed in Ice's cheeks and he looked down, shifting in the chair. "You're suggesting I let my free soul dominate?"

"It's worth a try," Nik said. "But Ice, there are always consequences to imbalance."

Ice raised his head and met Nik's eyes. "Consequences?"

"If your ego soul is suppressed, so is your reasoning and ability to act. Your body will do what comes naturally. It would be easy to lose control."

"Whoa," Ice blew out a heavy breath. "So I might…" His eyes grew wide.

Nik narrowed his eyes, scrutinizing his apprentice. "It could be a problem for some, but I know you well—aggression isn't part of your makeup. And remember, though your ego soul is diminished, it's there. If she resists, your reason should step forward."

Ice leaned his head down, covering his face with his hand. He exhaled loudly.

"If she's worth it, and feels the same about you, you'll work it out," Nik said. "Like all things, I imagine it gets easier with practice."

Ice groaned. Great.

He was willing to do what he had to in order to get closer to Jeni. It would be awkward, but he'd have to warn her.

Would she take the risk? That was the question.

✱ ✱ ✱

Jeni sat on her bed, propped up with pillows, book on her lap, thoughts elsewhere. After the fiasco today, she'd looked forward to chatting with Carolyn. But as her friend texted snippets of her day at work, Jeni realized she'd never be able to convey her feelings about the strange things happening here. Even a phone call would fall short. The events unfolding around her needed body language and eye-to-eye contact if the receiver might be expected to believe. No, this conversation would have to wait until she was home. So when Carolyn inevitably inquired about Ice, Jeni simply told her she'd given him the statue and let the subject drop.

A little while ago, not in the mood to put on a happy face, she'd declined joining the bonfire tonight. Her dad warned her that clouds were moving in the next day, bringing rain. "There probably won't be a fire tomorrow," he said.

"I'm okay with that, dad. You know too much campfire smoke gives me a headache." Though she did often get headaches from campfire smoke, tonight it was just an excuse so she could be alone.

She heard a light tapping on the door.

"Yeah?"

Her mom's face poked into the room. "Can I come in?"

"Sure."

"Just thought you might like a s'more. The stuff's outside by the fire. There's—"

"No thanks," Jeni interrupted.

"You might want to hear the end of what I was going to say…" her mom chided, eyebrows raised.

"Sorry, I'm just not very hungry. Go on."

"There's someone outside who asked to see you."

"Ice?" Jeni said in surprise.

"Uh-huh." Her mom gauged her reaction. "You don't seem as happy as I thought you'd be."

"I'm just surprised, that's all." Jeni scrambled to get her thoughts straight, sitting up and swinging her legs over the side of the bed. "I'll come out. Give me a minute."

Her mom paused at the door, studying Jeni with parental curiosity. Jeni had nothing to offer. She didn't even know how she felt about Ice right now. Her mom turned and left.

Jeni sat on the edge of the bed for a minute. She hadn't expected Ice to show up tonight. Tomorrow maybe. If she refused to see him, she'd have to provide an explanation. It would be much simpler to just go talk to him.

She paused by the kitchen window and noticed Ice standing at the edge of the campfire's glow, shifting from foot to foot. Grabbing a jacket, she quietly exited out the side door.

The light on the side of the cottage wasn't on and Jeni stepped into near blackness. She rushed around the corner, slowing once the fire was in sight. Ice looked up before she reached the flickering ring of light. He smiled a tight smile and intercepted her before the others noticed she was there. Except her mom. Jeni saw her watching.

"Hey," Ice said quietly. "I had to come and apologize. I couldn't leave things the way they ended at the hospital. I'm sorry."

Jeni looked at her feet. "I guess I should apologize too. I kinda lost it."

"Yeah, well, I get it—you were just trying to do what you thought was right. Nik's kinda old-school I guess. He likes to keep our business private."

Jeni glanced toward the group at the fire and inclined her head toward the beach. The water prohibited the absolute blackness of the surrounding area. Shades of gray robed the dock and boat. Ice nodded and they strolled in that direction. "You know," he said, "we decided not to report Kal's dad's disappearance."

"Why not?"

Ice shrugged. "We know what happened—there was an eye witness. The last thing we need is divers in the lake."

The thought of divers in the water brought forth the image of the creature's bestial tail as it smacked down on Nik's body and drew it into the depths. Jeni shuddered. Search and rescue would merely be feeding time.

"Cold?"

"No. Freaked." They stopped where the lawn ended and the sand began. Jeni glanced at Ice. "Ice, I thought about what Nik said, that he didn't have the statue in my dream because I hadn't given it to him yet. That's not exactly true. I'd given it to you. So why didn't you have it?"

"Mmmm."

"I'm afraid—" Jeni broke off and cleared her throat. "What if the premonition went farther into the future? What if something happened to the statue? Nik would still have to do something about the monster, right? What if that's what I saw?"

Ice turned to face her. "That's an awful lot of "what-ifs"." He smiled.

Her tightly wound emotions eased a bit in the warmth of his smile. She allowed a small laugh. "'Yeah, but do I have a point?"

He reached out, hesitated, and then cupped his palms under her elbows. An odd gesture until Jeni realized why he didn't take her hands: skin-to-skin contact.

"Premonitions are something to consider, but shouldn't be taken too literally. The farther into the future the event is, the more likely things will change."

Jeni nodded. Ice's explanation further alleviated her concern and her brain switched gears. The heat that spread from his hands felt full of promise.

"What I like," he said, running his fingers up her arms and back to her elbows, "is that you're worried about me." His touch sent tingles radiating up to the back of her neck and her breath caught in her throat as she watched him. The moonlight cast blue highlights on his hair and reflected chips of gray in his fragmented irises.

"I couldn't stand it if something happened to you…or anyone…because of me," Jeni said.

"You can't blame yourself for this. It just happened." He stared out into the darkness. "Some people believe they need to seek out their destiny; I believe destiny finds you. You had a part to play in this and you played it. Maybe it was time for you to discover who you really are."

Jeni sighed. "I'm glad you came back tonight."

Ice looked into her eyes. "I want to try something." Not waiting for a reply, he slid his hands down and gripped her hands. He watched her face curiously.

Jeni squeezed her eyes shut and then opened them slowly.

"Nothing?" Ice asked, grinning.

"Nothing," Jeni confirmed. "How come?"

Ice released her hands. "Here's the embarrassing part." Apprehension lined his forehead. "I have to… uh…give in to my instincts."

"What? What are you talking about?"

"To make it so you don't see visions when I touch you." He took a deep breath and moved closer. "It's kind of a long explanation, but now that we know it works I really just want to kiss you. Just promise to stop me if I cross a line."

Jeni frowned in confusion. His statement evoked at least a dozen questions, but apparently he didn't intend to let her ask any. He rested his hands on her shoulders for a moment then slid his fingers deftly up her neck to her jaw. "I trust your judgment," he murmured, and then brought his mouth down on hers.

Nervous and stiff, Jeni had one palm flat on his chest, ready to push him away at a moment's notice. But when his arms slid down around her waist and pulled her closer, her hands naturally migrated to the back of his neck. All her senses came alive. The softness of his hair caught in her fingers, the musky smell of his skin, the faint taste of cinnamon, the heat at the small of her back; they all coalesced into one sensory experience.

Lost in the moment, she had no idea when he slipped his hands under the edge of her shirt. Eventually though, she became cognizant of his hot fingers directly on her skin. She pulled back. "Ice," she whispered.

"Mmmm." He kissed her neck.

She extracted her fingers from his hair and moved her hands down to his biceps. His breath on her neck radiated shivers in every direction, and part of her asked why she wanted to stop him.

Because he trusted her judgment.

Jeni gently pushed away, taking a step back.

Ice straightened, dropping his hands to his sides. He had a wild, animalistic look in his eyes. Jeni watched warily, but the look soon faded. "Whoa," he exhaled.

Jeni gave him a shy smile. "We could sit by the fire."

"I'd like to, but I should go." He pulled his phone from his pocket. "Will you put your number in my phone? Maybe we can avoid any more miscommunication."

Though it seemed kind of pointless since tomorrow was her last day here, Jeni entered and saved her number. Maybe he would call or text her after she went home. Before returning his phone, she called her own number and then hung up so she'd have his number in her phone.

"There's something else I wanted to ask you about," Jeni said as she handed him his phone. "When you told me the legend of Itasca, didn't you mention someone who protected humans?"

"Nanabushu. Yeah, his father the West Wind sent him to earth to take care of the people. A lot of our myths are about him."

"So, if the monster is real, what about Nanabushu? Won't he…do something?"

"It's said that after the Europeans came, Nanabushu left."

"He left people to fend for themselves?"

"Well, he created the Thunderers to watch over us—spirits that travel with thunderstorms, in the form of huge, eagle-like birds. Thunderbirds."

"Oh. Like the car."

Ice chuckled. "Well, the symbolism is taken from our lore. Anyway, spring through fall, thunderstorms come through to look after us. Only the Thunderers can defeat the underwater manitou."

"But they haven't defeated him yet?"

"Sure they have. But he always comes back."

"Always?"

"Always."

"Like a psycho killer in a slasher movie," she muttered. Ice chuckled, but Jeni was thoughtful. "So, can you ask the Thunderers to help you?"

"I'm sure Nik's planning on it."

"Good."

"I'm picking Nik up at the hospital first thing in the morning. I'm not sure what's going to happen after that. But I'll see you sometime tomorrow," he assured her.

"Promise?"

"Promise." Ice dipped his head and barely brushed her lips with his. Jeni watched as the darkness swallowed his retreat.

Suddenly, a s'more sounded awesome. Only two of Jeni's aunts remained at the fire and they appeared deep in conversation. Since they might not have known that Ice was ever here, there was a good possibility she wouldn't get caught in an uncomfortable discussion.

In the middle of toasting her marshmallow, Jeni heard footsteps and looked up. Oh, fabulous. Tyler entered the ring of light and sat down one chair away from her. As much as she hated a half-toasted marshmallow, Jeni contemplated slapping the s'more together and taking it in the house.

Then to her dismay, her aunts got up. "Should we leave the s'more stuff?"

Both she and Tyler shook their heads.

Once the sliding glass door slid shut, her cousin turned to her.

Jeni hastily assembled the s'more. A weak plan, but it was all she had. It was hard to talk and eat at the same time.

"So?"

"So what?" Jeni crunched into the treat.

"Why was he here? What did he say?"

She took her time chewing and swallowing. "It's none of your business."

"Wrong. This morning it was none of my business, but if you remember correctly, you dragged me into your business. I must've been nuts to agree not to tell anyone about this…this…craziness, because now I feel responsible for your safety. And I need to be sure that you're not going ghost hunting with this dude."

Jeni took another bite, reflecting that it was impossible to eat a s'more slowly since it crumbled as soon as you bit into it.

Oh how she regretted asking Tyler to drive her to the hospital. What had she been thinking? Now he was right, as long as he kept her secret, she had to tell him what he wanted to know. Jeni sighed, licking her lips. "He came to apologize. They're going to handle the situation. Without me."

He gave a curt nod. "Hey, Jeni?" The accusatory tone was gone and replaced with genuine curiosity, which compelled Jeni to meet his gaze. "Do you believe all this stuff about a monster on the loose and you being a priestess or whatever?"

In his car at the hospital, they didn't have a discussion; it was more like a confession. Jeni had alternately blurted out and choked on the story. When she was finished, Tyler started the car and drove back without a word—probably fearing if he pushed the conversation any further, she would lose it. His perception was correct; her emotions had balanced precariously on the knife-edge of control.

"All I know," she said in a low voice, "is when I shook Ice's hand I saw some kind of vision. And then the dream I had—with the stone—I've never had a dream so vivid; so realistic. I'm definitely going to investigate our family's roots when I get home."

She sat back in the chair and popped the last bite of s'more in her mouth, asking herself what she did believe. "As far as an underwater monster or spirit, as they call it..." she shook her head, "I don't know what to think. But I had a weird dizzy spell when I fell in the water that day. And a man has died. And Nik..." she shrugged, "...They believe it Tyler. They take it very seriously. So I guess I'd have to say I do believe—because they do."

Tyler stared at her for a minute, as if trying to read her mind. Then he broke eye contact and stared into the fire.

Jeni considered her sticky hands. As she opened her mouth to say she was heading inside, her phone rang. Licking her fingers, Jeni pulled the phone from her pocket.

Ice? She shot a glance at Tyler. This was going to be awkward.

What you see with your eyes shut is what counts.

—Lame Deer, Lakota

CHAPTER 9

About ten minutes after Ice left the resort he got a call from Nik. The medicine man didn't bother with a hello or any other pleasantries. "Did you give the dream stone back to that girl?" he demanded.

"No." The exasperation in the medicine man's voice took Ice by surprise. "The last time I saw it was in your room at the hospital. It was on the nightstand."

Nik swore. "It's not here. But that's not the worst news. Ice, the stone figure is gone."

"Gone?"

"Stolen. Had to be. It was wrapped in a cloth, in my duffle bag, under some clothes. Obviously, someone was looking for it."

"Who?"

"Who else knew about the statue?"

Ice thought for a minute. Roffe from the Gas and Go? No, that was ludicrous.

Nik answered for him. "The manitou."

Ice felt like a rock dropped in his stomach. "But… how…" he sputtered.

"He's a spirit of the water realm; the statue was in the water. He felt its power when it roused him from years of slumber."

"But Nik, the manitou couldn't have stolen the statue from your room."

"You're right about that. But the creature's cunning has always made him a formidable foe; he can be most persuasive. Many humans have fallen for his promises, not realizing until it was too late that they would pay a price greater than they'd imagined. Regardless of the bargain's clever wording, the monster's currency is always human life."

"Someone is helping him." The vast ramifications of the statement overwhelmed Ice's ability to consider each possibility. The monster's reach was no longer limited by water. His wrath could be anywhere; touch anyone. Ice's heart rate quickened and each beat sent fear radiating through his veins. "What—" he choked, "what are we going to do?"

"Nothing right now. I have to assume whoever took the statue also took the dream stone. Any plan we come up with might be foretold. Already we've lost our first line of defense; we can't afford to lose the element of surprise as well."

Ice groaned.

"Don't forget, medicine stones can only be used by someone with a link to the spirit world. The chances that the manitou found such a person so quickly are slim. But if the dream stone is used, we'll know because it'll return to me. Truthfully, that would be the best scenario. Once the stone is back in my possession, we can plan without fear of our strategy being discovered. Also, I may derive clues from the stone about who has used it and where it's been."

"And if it doesn't come back?"

"That's trickier. I can formulate plausible scenarios but I can't choose nor share the plan of action with you until the moment before we execute."

"So we're in a holding pattern."

"Exactly. It's a waiting game. You might as well get some sleep. I'll call you if the stone returns."

"Okay." Ice ended the call but didn't put the phone down. The thought of someone out there doing the monster's bidding unnerved him. The statue wasn't the only thing in the water that day. Jeni bled in the river. What had Nik said about the manitou's vengeance? He'd go after the bloodline of his captors. Knowing the power that woke him could also subdue him…wouldn't the creature also try to eliminate those who might try to capture him now? With the statue taken out of play, would the manitou be after Jeni next?

Ice didn't know what his chances were of getting Jeni on the phone, but it was worth a try.

"What, you wanted to make sure I gave you my real number?"

The sound of her voice steadied him somewhat and Ice managed a laugh. "No. Why? Did you consider it?"

"Not for a second."

"Hey," Ice's voice got serious, "I guess this could've waited until tomorrow, but I feel really bad about it."

"About what?"

"I just spoke to Nik…uh…I'm really sorry Jeni. Your statue has disappeared."

"What do you mean disappeared?"

"Stolen. Nik had it with him at the hospital… hidden. Someone was looking for it."

"Why wo…body want…would know?

"Jeni, you're breaking up."

"Ice can…ar me?"

"I'm barely getting anything. I don't know if you can hear me, but I'll see you tomorrow."

Ice looked at his phone. The call was dropped.

Shoot. He would've liked to warn her to be extra careful. But at least he knew she was safe at the cottage for tonight.

❋ ❋ ❋

"The reception here sucks," Jeni said as she moved closer to the fire. She might have been able to talk to Ice a little longer if she'd been willing to venture out in the dark, but she'd only made it just outside the circle of the fire's glow.

She knew Ice was in his car though, and since the connection was clear at first, she thought he might be driving out of range anyway.

"I know. I have to stand on the dock to use my phone." With a large stick, Tyler spread out the remaining logs from the fire.

Jeni expected him to go in after she took the call. She wouldn't admit it out loud, but she was glad he stayed. "I gotta wash my sticky hands."

"Yeah, the fire will just burn itself out now."

Jeni went straight for the bathroom. She rinsed her hands and then hopped in the shower. The hot water on her back made her think of Ice's hands and a warm flush swelled inside her. Then she thought about his call.

By the time she finished drying her hair, she'd made a decision. She put on her pajamas, got into bed, and turned out the light. No reading tonight, she had other plans. Sliding a hand under her pillow, Jeni curled her fingers around the dream stone.

At the hospital, furious with both Ice and Nik, she'd made sure her jacket hit the nightstand, and snatched up the blue stone. She didn't intend to use it; she just wanted her collateral back.

Had she thought of it when Ice was here, she would've given it back to him. Fortunately she hadn't remembered the stone until she was in the shower, because now that her statue was gone she wondered if her premonition might be accurate. If she slept with the stone tonight, would she have the same dream?

Nik and Ice couldn't ignore the warning if she had the same dream twice.

But it wasn't the same.

Jeni was at the site of the car wreck outside Itasca State Park that she'd seen with her dad and uncle on the way to the Wilderness Drive. She recognized the speed limit sign the car had barely missed and saw the large white scar left on the tree, where the vehicle had struck. The car, though, was gone.

A blue light bobbed at the edge of the woods, waiting for her. She turned and followed it into the trees.

There was no path as she made her way through the forest, but the plump crescent moon, high in the clear sky, helped light the way. She emerged onto a blacktop road. The light floated on the other side and she crossed to pursue it. Not much farther along, the light stopped moving. Jeni advanced toward it, expecting it to continue on its way. The light simply hovered. She looked around, noted the large amount of logs scattered on the ground, then spied something else.

A trap door.

The blue glow hung directly over the door in the forest floor and then slipped through a crack into the space below. Jeni grasped the metal ring and lifted the door. It opened easily and without a sound. She kneeled at the edge to look inside.

The space appeared to be an old cellar. The light flitted around the small chamber, coming to rest in a corner.

In the area illuminated by the light, Jeni saw a stone—a shape she recognized.

Feline. Horned.

The underwater manitou.

The statue!

Without thinking, she dropped inside the space. Its walls were made of stone and dirt, but the blue light cast an ethereal glow.

Crouching down, Jeni reached for the stone figure. But just as she was unable to pull Ice from the jaws of the underwater monster, she couldn't pick up the statue. Her hand passed through it.

"No…" Jeni cried, recoiling as her voice split the silence.

The sound woke her up. She stayed still for a

moment, wondering if she woke her grandma. At first all she could hear was her own pounding heart, but eventually she detected even breathing from the other bed. Propping herself up on an elbow, Jeni reached for her book light on the nightstand and clicked it on.

She breathed deeply, replaying the dream in her head.

Though she knew the stone was gone, she looked under her pillow then pulled back the covers and got out of bed. The dream stone had shown her where the statue was or where it would be and then returned to its master. She'd call Ice first thing tomorrow and they'd find the trap door in the woods.

She got back in bed feeling rather pleased with herself. Her gaze drifted toward the window. A slice of moon cut across the black strip of glass at the edge of the shade. If they retrieved the statue, the first premonition couldn't come to fruition. Jeni stared at the ceiling, recalling the dream from the night before.

Suddenly she sat up and her eyes snapped to the window. Crawling to the end of the bed, she drew the shade back and looked into the sky—a replica of the sky in her dream tonight.

In her first dream the sky was cloudy. The distant lightning and wind promised a thunderstorm on the way. The same weather her dad said was coming tomorrow.

The statue was there right now.

And Jeni knew how to find the cellar.

Hold on a minute. If it were there now, it would still be there in the morning. What was she thinking? Go out in the dark in the middle of the night by herself?

No way.

She wouldn't.

She *couldn't.*

Jeni didn't lie back down.

She knew if she closed her eyes she'd see Ice's limp body hanging from the monster's mouth.

Tonight's dream didn't show her and Ice finding the statue in the daylight, it showed her, by herself, at night. There must be a reason why. Unfortunately the only reason Jeni could think of is that the statue would no longer be there in the morning.

How could she shrug this off? She had to know. Had to see if there really was a cellar. And if so, was the statue there?

Her mind flicked to Tyler.

No. Not after today.

She had to do this herself or forget about it.

Squeezing her eyes shut, she pictured Ice. The way his face lit up when he saw her. His easy smile. The sincerity reflected in his blue eyes when he spoke.

Without making any conscious decision about what she was doing, Jeni peeled her pajama bottoms off and slid out of bed. Fortunately her jeans were on top of the pile of clothes on her suitcase. She slipped them on, picked up her purse from the floor, and retrieved her reading light from the nightstand.

Still allowing herself to think of only her current action, she entered the kitchen and shone her light around the room, searching for her mom's purse. She needed the car keys.

Shoot.

She did not want to sneak into her parents' room.

Her gaze fell on her dad's jacket, hanging from a hook. He always left the keys in his pocket. When she hurried over and squeezed the bottom of the jacket, her right hand was rewarded with a heavy lump. She snaked her hand inside the pocket and extracted the keys, then slipped into her shoes and fleece jacket.

Despite her best efforts to fool herself, Jeni's heart was hammering in her chest by the time her hand grasped the doorknob. She took a deep, calming breath, but it rushed out in ragged bursts, exposing rather than abating her terror.

She wasn't sure how long she stood there, hand on the doorknob, eyes closed, summoning the courage to leave the cottage. Finally, she slowly rotated the knob, only opening her eyes when the latch was free of the doorjamb. With just enough room for her to slip through, she quickly stepped out and eased the door closed behind her. At the back corner of the cottage, the motion sensor light blazed into action causing relief and alarm in equal measure.

Jeni hurried to the car and got in, barely latching the door. The lingering smell of her mom's hand cream and the faint fast food odor held a tiny amount of comfort. Holding her breath, she turned the key in the ignition. Without waiting to see if the noise woke anyone, she shifted into reverse and backed out onto the gravel road. In drive, she hardly touched the gas pedal with her trembling foot as the car slowly crept from the cottage.

When she reached the blacktop, Jeni opened her door, swung it shut tight, and hit the power lock button. She pulled out, not daring to contemplate the inky shapes looming on both sides of the road.

Her heart thumped madly, every breath a struggle. Jeni fought the urge to slam on the brakes and turn around.

Maybe she could call Ice, ask him to meet her there. Phone in hand, she looked at the car's clock. How could she possibly know what time it had been when she saw the statue in the cellar? She leaned forward, looking up through the windshield for the moon. It was nearly overhead—just like in her dream.

She deemed how their conversation would go. Ice would either try to talk her out of it or he'd ask her to wait for him. Jeni peered up at the moon again. There wasn't time to wait.

She set the phone on the console.

After turning left on Highway 200, she watched for the east park entrance. Once past it, she slowed the car to a crawl, looking for the telltale road sign on the opposite side. Glancing in the rear view mirror, she noticed distant headlights. Maybe she should be relieved she wasn't the only one out here, but she didn't need someone asking questions, or noticing she was a girl, alone in the middle of the night.

There! The sign. Passing by, she twisted in the seat to confirm it was a speed limit sign then carefully guided the car to a stop, as far off the road as possible. The approaching headlights grew larger.

Jeni contemplated the dark forest across the road, frozen in fear. So much blackness against her one, small light. What was she doing? Wasn't there someone more qualified for this task?

She might have lost her nerve right then, but

the oncoming car spurred her into action. If someone noticed her sitting here, they might stop. It would be better if the car looked abandoned.

Jeni stuffed the car keys into her purse and zipped it shut. She swung the door open, blinked when the interior lights came on, then quickly hit the lock button and closed it, peering down the road. The other car was still a ways off. She hurried across the road.

An overwhelming feeling of déjà-vu enveloped her as she clambered through the ditch to the edge of the woods; she half-expected to see the blue light. It appeared she was on her own though, so she stepped into the trees and clicked on her light.

Jeni wasn't sure which was worse, the gloom in which she could see the shadowed shapes around her, or the complete blackness surrounding the small island of light. Her heart chugged at breakneck speed like a train about to derail. She must be crazy to be out here.

She paused for a moment to study her return path. The moon, nearly half-full, was enough to light the road and the speed limit sign. She pressed forward, almost panting. Forcing one foot in front of the other, Jeni visualized herself returning to the car with the statue in hand; imagined how it would feel to present the statue to Ice the next day.

Relief washed over her when she emerged onto the blacktop road and realized it was probably the main park drive. She scurried across. The site shouldn't be much further, and if she didn't find the door, or the cellar, then the dream was just a dream.

Flinching at every rustle of leaves, Jeni imagined

eyes following her from beyond her ring of light. Rather than direct the beam toward the noises, she rushed forward, afraid of what she might reveal.

Her light fell on an overgrown log. She lifted the small beam higher and saw more logs ahead.

She was there. Stepping into the clearing, she moved her light from one log to another, recognizing that not only were they uniformly sized, but also strewn about in a rough rectangle. Included in the outline was a tall, dark structure. Closer inspection revealed a crumbling chimney built of stone.

This must be the remains of a cabin. That's why there was a cellar here.

The triumph at finding a place she'd only seen in a dream was quickly overshadowed by the thought that everything she dreamed the first time might also be accurate. She was here to make sure that wouldn't happen.

Hurrying now, Jeni searched the ground for the trap door.

It wasn't hard to find. Leaves, sticks, and dirt were pushed into piles around the door—evidence that someone had recently unearthed the cellar's entrance.

Jeni paused. She'd been running purely on emotion—afraid that if she thought too much about what she was doing she'd lose her nerve. As she studied the door, which had clearly been uncovered within the past few days, a little bit of reason crept through her gut reactions.

Someone uncovered the cellar.

Someone stole the statue.

What if that someone was inside the cellar — right now?

She certainly hadn't been concerned with stealth as she approached. If someone was down there, they knew she was here. Jeni turned and shuffled away, making her retreat obvious. At the edge of the clearing, she clicked her light off and stepped behind a tree.

Why didn't she keep going? All the way to the car?

She had to know, that's why. If this place, the trap door, and the cellar all existed, wasn't it possible the statue was in there? Besides, in her dream, no one had been inside the cellar.

Jeni peeped around the tree and waited until she couldn't take it anymore. She just wanted to get the statue and get out of there.

She dropped her purse next to the trap door, grasped the ring, and pulled. The door lifted slightly, but it was heavy! In dreamland she'd thrown it open as if it weighed nothing.

Setting her light down, Jeni put both hands on the ring and yanked with all her might. As the door came up, she leaned back and used her body weight to keep the momentum. Once it passed ninety degrees, she lost control and the door slammed open, knocking her on her butt.

Jeni crawled to her light and snatched it up. She directed it into the cellar, getting on her feet and stepping away warily. It looked exactly as she'd dreamed. Nothing moved, no one jumped out, so she edged closer and aimed the beam into the corner where the statue would be.

Puzzled, she got down on her hands and knees to

shed more light on whatever was there.

It wasn't the statue; it looked like cloth. A small bundle of cloth.

Disappointed, Jeni started to back away and stopped. Could the statue be wrapped in the cloth?

Was she grasping at straws?

She'd come this far.

Inspecting the interior of the space with her light, Jeni didn't see any kind of stairs or ladder. And without the benefit of the ethereal blue light, the hole in the earth was downright spooky. She rested the beam on the cloth, thinking.

Adrenaline fueled; determined to finish her business and leave, Jeni got up and searched the ground. It didn't take long to find what she sought, a long branch. She dragged it to the cellar, and lying down on her stomach, she held her light in one hand and the branch in the other.

By stretching her arm out she could just touch the cloth. Wriggling forward until she hung slightly in the opening, she reached out again and caught the fabric on the end of the branch. She pulled sideways, attempting to lift the cloth, but it slipped off. She scooted slightly forward and tried again.

When Jeni hooked the cloth this time, she gave it a yank, knocking herself off balance. One leg instinctively came up, shifting her body's center of gravity forward. She teetered for a second with her arms waving wildly, but the recently upturned leaves were damp and slippery, and she slid, head first, into the cellar.

✶ ✶ ✶

Ice woke in confusion. He was on the couch, TV on low volume. Then he remembered. Unable to stop his mind from conjuring horrible scenarios—most where either Jeni or Nik ended up dead—he'd hoped the empty-headed bliss of television might give him some rest. Apparently it worked.

But what woke him up?

Music sounded, muffled and tinny. His phone. Where the heck was it? He was sure he'd set it right next to the pillow his head was on. Probing into the couch's crevices, he finally located the device between the cushion and arm. The number was unfamiliar, but local. As he pushed the receive button Ice noticed he'd already missed a call.

"H'lo?" he pushed the hair out of his eyes and peered at the clock on the DVD player.

"Ice?" a gruff voice asked.

"Yeah, this is Ice. Who's this?"

"Hanson Greenleaf. Glad you picked up. I've already tried Nik—a few times—with no luck. Then when you didn't answer, I really got to worrying. Anyway, I know it's late, but I've got something you and Nik need to know."

Hanson wasn't a tribe elder, but he was a respected long-time member of the community. If he'd taken the effort to track down Ice—at this time of night—he had something important to say.

"Nik had to spend the night in the hospital, that's why you couldn't get him," Ice explained. "I'm picking him up in the morning though, what's up?"

"Robin can't sleep most nights on account of her arthritis, so she sits up and watches TV with the police scanner on in the background. There's been an accident at Lake Itasca."

Ice frowned. If Hanson's wife heard it on the scanner, the man couldn't possibly be talking about Kal's dad. "What kind of accident?" Anxiety immediately woke in his chest, flexing its tendrils.

"A girl disappeared."

The man's words transformed Ice's unease into alarm. He pressed his lips together and breathed deeply through his nose. No—the dreams he'd been having when the phone woke him up were freaking him out. He had no reason to think Jeni was out at Lake Itasca in the middle of the night.

"You know they don't go into much detail over the radio, but it sounds like there was a witness," Hanson continued his account. "A boy who was with her swears something pulled her under water. After what happened this morning, I figured this couldn't be coincidental."

That Hanson knew about Kal's dad didn't surprise Ice. They'd kept the news from the authorities, not the tribe. People needed to be wary. "Ah crap," he sighed, dropping his shoulders and relaxing his grip on the phone. A girl and a guy. Not Jeni. "Thanks Hanson. I'll let Nik know right away."

"Ayup. Watch yourself out there. He isn't kidding around—he's out for blood."

"I know." Ice shuddered at the chill that crawled up his spine at Hanson's words. The man was so careful about not speaking any of the monster's names; Ice knew he was spooked. "I'll be careful. Thanks again."

Drawing in a deep breath, Ice willed his pulse to return to normal. A couple—it'd been a couple, not just a girl. Suddenly the waning tendrils of anxiety sprang back to life and wrapped around his heart, squeezing hard. In his mind's eye Ice saw Jeni climb into Tyler's car. Ice had mistaken him for Jeni's boyfriend.

Tyler had also driven her to the hospital.

Ice stood and shook his head as if to clear the conflicting thoughts racing through it. Good grief, he was paranoid! What he should be doing is trying to get a hold of Nik.

He tried Nik's number. As expected, the call went immediately to voice mail. Ice muttered a curse and went in his bedroom to boot up his computer.

The hospital's automated switchboard let him enter Nik's room number, but the call went unanswered. The phones may be silenced at night, or perhaps the volume was so low Nik didn't hear it.

The only way to deliver the news to Nik was to go to the hospital in person—something he'd planned to do in a few hours anyway. There was no point in rushing off, Ice reasoned. As long as the authorities were on the scene, his and Nik's hands were tied. He swiveled in his chair to face the bed and gazed at it despairingly, knowing he'd simply lie there and imagine horrible scenarios. Instead, he headed for the shower, wondering how to talk his way past the hospital lobby attendant.

There is a road in the hearts of all of us,
hidden and seldom traveled,
which leads to an unknown, secret place.

—Chief Luther Standing Bear, Lakota

CHAPTER 10

Jeni landed hard, on her back. The painful jolt spread from her core to her limbs, and a crushing weight deflated her lungs. She opened her mouth to inhale, but her chest didn't want to expand. She gasped for breath, panic pushing aside reason.

Oh God, she'd broken her spine and was going to die here in this dark hole!

Her gasps and wheezes became more frantic and her vision grew fuzzy at the edges. The awful sounds she made sounded strangely familiar though she knew she'd never made them before. As she struggled for breath, the memory surfaced.

Video—it was a video on YouTube her dad made her watch. A woman stomping grapes slipped and fell on her back. She'd had the wind knocked out of her and sounded just like Jeni did now.

Pushing the panic away, Jeni took little shallow breaths. She twisted her body slightly and convinced herself that her spine wasn't broken. With each inhalation she brought in a bit more air. Her head cleared and she pushed herself up to her elbows, finally able to breathe through her nose.

Her face wrinkled at the conflicting smells. The musty stench of decay was at odds with the scent of fresh dirt and a smoky, sulfurous odor.

Though she wanted to scramble out of the dark, dank chamber, she forced herself to stay still and breathe for a few more minutes. Her light had landed nearby and was on, but the surrounding blackness pressed in on the small island of light, trying to shrink it into oblivion. Unable to endure it any longer, Jeni crawled to her light and flashed it around the cellar.

The space was maybe eight foot square. She trained the light on a tunnel dug into a sidewall. It looked as though it had caved in. The site provided a reason for the smell of fresh dirt and confirmed what she'd determined earlier—someone had been here recently. Jeni shuddered.

A shovel, tarp, and rope lay near the tunnel as well as a few empty plastic bottles and food wrappers. An old stove or furnace occupied the far wall. In the corner nearby lay the cloth that got her into this predicament in the first place.

The statue had better be in it.

Convinced she was going to be okay, Jeni rose shakily to her feet, testing her range of movement. She knew she'd feel this tomorrow.

Crouching down, she covered the cloth with her hand and closed her fist. She groaned out loud.

Nothing. It was empty.

She made a quick survey of the rest of the area, hesitantly checking behind the furnace and under the tarp; kicking around in a mound of dirt in case the statue was buried.

Mission failed.

Time to get out of here.

Jeni clenched her light in her teeth and reached up to the opening. She grasped the ledge and attempted to haul herself up. Yeah, that wasn't going to happen. It might have been possible when she was ten and could make it all the way across the monkey bars, but not today.

Relief that she'd survived the fall had overcome her other fears momentarily, but they returned quickly along with the edge of hysteria.

Jeni approached the furnace and gave it a shove with both hands. It didn't budge.

She couldn't get out.

Now she started to freak out.

She frantically flashed her light around. The only other idea she had was to pile dirt under the opening. Just enough to make her tall enough to climb out. She grabbed the shovel and went to work. The scraping sounds were almost comforting in the muffled stillness of the cellar.

Jeni froze with a load of dirt on the end of the shovel. She thought she heard something.

The rustle of leaves.

Animal?

Hungry animal?

Psychopathic serial killer?

The dirt rained off the end of the shovel and she noticed her arms were shaking.

As the sound grew closer, Jeni became convinced

it was a person walking. Her heart fluttered crazily because she knew who it was.

It was not a kind stranger who happened to be walking through the woods in the middle of the night and would rescue her.

The swishing of leaves picked up pace. And grew nearer.

It was the statue-stealing, tunnel-digging, cellar occupant, and Jeni had to assume the person would not be happy to see her there.

Without a sound, she bent down to retrieve her light and switched it off while backing away from the open trap door. The shovel remained in her hand. Her back touched the wall and she scooted over to the furnace, attempting to jam herself into the small space behind it.

A light flickered across the opening overhead.

The footsteps stopped.

Jeni pressed her lips together and bit down on them to keep any sound from escaping.

Light illuminated the inside of the cellar.

She tried to make herself as small as possible.

"Jeni?"

Wait. What?

Relief flooded over her and she ran from her hiding place.

A beam of light washed over her, making her squint.

"What the hell?" Tyler exclaimed, kneeling on the ground.

"How did you find me? Never mind, just get me out! I can't get out!"

He sat back on his heels. "Fortunately I saw your purse up here—that was the only breadcrumb I had," he replied, exasperated. "I can't believe you looked me right in the eye and said you weren't going ghost hunting."

"I'm not!" Jeni extended her hands toward him. "Just pull me out and I'll explain everything."

Tyler set his flashlight on the lip of the opening, reached down, and grasped her by the upper arms.

He leaned back to hoist her up and suddenly he pitched forward. He let her go and she stumbled backwards as he hit the ground in front of her.

Oh no! She'd pulled him in too!

Then a black object catapulted through the opening and landed on Tyler's leg. He scrambled to get back on his feet. "What was that!" he yelled.

"You must've knocked my purse in…" Jeni started, but trailed off when she realized it didn't make any sense.

Before either of them could fathom what had just happened; the trap door slammed shut overhead.

"Hey!" Tyler shouted. "Let us out of here!"

His flashlight lay on its side, still on. The glow was enough for Jeni to see the shock and confusion on her cousin's face transform into horror, as he comprehended the noises from above.

Her heart stopped. "What's happening?" she whispered.

It sounded as if something heavy bumped and scraped across the door. "Logs," Tyler said.

After two more heavy thumps the forest above went silent.

They were trapped.

Imprisoned.

Already stretched to the breaking point, Jeni's courage finally shattered. Her eyes darted wildly, taking in the suffocating blackness surrounding the miniscule beam of light.

"This is all your fault!" It came out like a hiss between her teeth. Anger was better than the panic that threatened to crush her.

Tyler stopped pounding the door with his fist. He flicked the light in her direction. "My fault?" She could see his eyes narrow. "I followed you here—trying to protect you! You promised if I didn't tell your parents what's been going on that you wouldn't go ghost hunting."

"I'm not ghost hunting. I...I thought the statue would be here."

"What? The statue!" His face crumpled in disbelief. "Your statue has apparently already caused more trouble than it's worth."

"Exactly. And I never would've bought it if you hadn't badgered me into going for a drive with you!" As much as Jeni wished it were true, words spoken earlier echoed in denial: *Destiny finds you. Things happen for a reason.*

Tyler certainly wasn't buying her rationale. "That's a bunch of crap." He'd given up banging on the door and searched the small space for another way out.

Jeni sank to the ground, knowing her cousin's search was futile. She wrapped her arms around her legs, chin resting on her knees.

Tyler grabbed her by the shoulder and she winced under his glowering stare. "What the hell is going on?" he demanded.

"I don't know," Jeni choked out, the anger draining away as her eyes filled with tears. "I had this dream…" she began and swiped at a tear with the back of her finger.

She blurted it all out. Taking the dream stone from the hospital. Ice's call telling her the statue had been stolen. Her dream about the cellar.

Relaying it all to Tyler renewed Jeni's purpose and helped restore her nerve. She took a deep breath and exhaled in a rush. At least she wasn't alone down here.

Tyler squatted down and searched her face with angry eyes. "The only reason I'll give this dream of yours any merit is because we've been trapped down here intentionally. I don't know if your statue was ever hidden here, but it's hard to believe some freak just decided it would be fun to shut us in. Although it happens in the movies all the time," he added with a mirthless smile.

Tyler rose and reached into his jacket pocket. He handed Jeni his cell phone. "Call Jake." He trained his light on the collapsed tunnel, and moved to inspect it closely.

Jeni brought up his contacts list before she realized his phone showed no service. "Ugh! Of course, no service. I can try mine," she said dubiously.

She dug through her purse. Twice. Then used her light to see inside and piled most of the contents on her lap. Her phone wasn't there. She thought back to the last time she'd used it and then it dawned on her.

She hadn't used it, just held it in her hand and then changed her mind. On the way here. She'd set it down on the console in the car and was certain it was still there now.

"I left mine in the car," she said miserably.

Tyler rolled his eyes at her. "Perfect." He held a long hefty branch in one hand. It was bigger than the one Jeni had used to poke the cloth bundle. "Let's see if we can lift the door with this."

Jeni held the light while Tyler braced the branch against the door and shoved.

The door bumped slightly up and then back down. After repeated tries, it was clear that the logs on top were too heavy.

Tyler dropped the branch and went to the tunnel. "I don't know if this goes anywhere, but there's only one way to find out." He passed the light to Jeni and picked up the shovel to jab at the loose dirt.

He froze when he heard a noise above them. Scratching.

Jeni directed the beam of light toward the sound. Fragments of some kind drifted from the crack along the edge of the door. She squatted down to examine the debris. "Wood shavings."

They shouted to whoever was up there, pleading to be set free, but bits of wood continued to sift down until they could see the tip of a knife protruding slightly from the rough hole.

"Look, we don't know who you are or what you look like. Roll the logs off and go—we'll never be able to identify you," Tyler attempted to reason with their jailer.

The knife was removed from the hole, something else took its place, and then an engine started. The smell of exhaust rushed into the cellar. Tyler's eyes went wide. "He's gassing us. Holy shit! Someone's trying to kill us!"

He grabbed a handful of dirt and packed it into the hole, but the sandy, loose soil wouldn't stay and kept raining back to the ground.

Feeling helpless, Jeni peered frantically around the small area. Her gaze settled on the furnace. She pointed the light in that direction, ignoring Tyler's muffled protest. He had his arm crossed over his nose in order to breathe through his sleeve. With his attention now on the duct that protruded from the furnace, Jeni moved the beam of light along the conduit to the cellar ceiling.

"Do you think that goes up to the chimney?" Jeni asked.

"What chimney?"

Jeni pointed up. "There's a stone chimney up there."

Tyler rushed over and cranked the lever to open the hatch used to feed the furnace. The shaft fell off in his hand. His attempt to pry the door up with his fingers wasn't going well, so Jeni grabbed her purse. She carried it over by him. "I have a pocket knife," she said. She knew exactly where to find it and within seconds it was in his hand.

Jeni squatted with one hand on the floor to steady herself, her other arm crossed over her face. Her head buzzed. She watched as Tyler pried the steel plate up and snapped the inside of the broken latch. He swung the door open and stuck his face inside.

When he withdrew his head and turned to her, she could see a glimmer of hope in his eyes. "Take off your jacket," he said, and motioned her over.

She slipped out of her jacket and kneeled next to him. "Put your face in, and stuff your jacket around it," he instructed.

As soon as her nose reached the opening, she smelled the acrid smoky smell of a fireplace. It was a welcome change from the stifling exhaust. When her face was fully inside, she noticed something else: fresh air.

Tyler put his head next to hers and they filled the rest of the space with their jackets, in an attempt to seal their faces inside the furnace. The outlet to the chimney above was no doubt clogged with webs, nests and other debris, but it wasn't completely blocked.

Jeni sagged as her head swam. Tyler put his arm around her and braced his hand against the furnace, holding her in place. She was too grateful to dwell on how creepy it was to have her cousin's arm around her.

"How long will we have to stay like this?" Jeni mumbled.

"I don't know. Until whatever it is runs out of gas. The good thing is, it doesn't sound like a car running. It's something smaller."

Jeni didn't reply; her spinning head was making her sick to her stomach.

She concentrated on breathing the fresh air.

THUNDERSTONE

*** * ***

As Ice stepped from the darkness into a pool of light at the hospital entrance, he approached the door purposefully, hoping he looked distracted and desperate—the latter not far from the truth.

"My grandpa asked me to come right away," he blurted at the woman behind the desk without stopping. He didn't bother with the elevator either, in case the woman came after him. He hit the stairs and climbed them two at a time.

On the second floor, he waited in the stairwell until the nurse on duty left for her rounds then he silently padded down the hall to Nik's room. Soft snores rumbled from the bed. Enough light spilled into the room for him to make out the outline of Nik's prone form.

Ice shook the medicine man's shoulder. "Nik," he whispered.

Nik stirred, snorted, and then resumed snoring.

Ice used a little more force, but kept his voice low. "Hey. Nik."

The medicine man rolled to his back and opened his eyes. "Ice?" He glanced from side to side. "Am I awake?"

Unable to suppress a smile, Ice nodded. "I hope so. I have news." His face went slack. "It's not good."

Nik passed his hand over his face and started to push himself up.

"Here," Ice said, pressing the button to lift the top of the bed.

"Light?" The older man waved his hand toward

the small fixture above his head.

Ice flipped the switch on the reading light. "Hanson called me a little while ago when he couldn't get you." He kept his voice low; one ear attuned to the hallway. "His wife heard an incident on her police scanner. A girl disappeared on Lake Itasca—in Lake Itasca," he clarified.

Nik frowned and shook his head. "Now it's more urgent than ever that we act, yet we're forced to do nothing until search and rescue teams are out of the area."

"What are we—" Ice broke off and turned his head toward the doorway. With his finger in front of his lips, he silently backed into the bathroom. Seconds later, the nurse entered.

"Can't sleep, hon? Are you having any pain?"

"No, I'm fine," Nik answered. "I'm just looking forward to sleeping in my own bed."

While she attended Nik, Ice moved behind the bathroom door so he could peer through the crack. He was looking directly at the nightstand, where the nurse shifted things around.

"I'll bring you some fresh water."

"Thank you," Nik said.

Ice remained behind the door hoping she'd return right away, rather than leave him wondering if she was going to walk in at any moment. He waited, listening to the soft hum of equipment and monitors and breathing shallowly to avoid a nose-full of the harsh disinfectant used to clean the bathroom. His eyes travelled idly over the items on the nightstand.

His heart stopped. Was that—? He smushed his

face into the crack of the door, attempting to see better in the dim light. It looked liked the dream stone was on Nik's nightstand. Did it just return? Had it been there when he walked in? Did Nik know it was there?

Ice shifted from foot to foot. He opened his mouth to whisper through the crack, then closed it and pressed flat against the wall. Footsteps in the hall.

"Here you go, sugar."

Nik thanked the nurse while she fussed for what seemed an eternity to Ice. He forced himself to wait another thirty seconds after her footfalls had faded, then he stepped back into Nik's room. He picked up the stone and held his open palm out to Nik. "Did you know it was back?"

The medicine man's wide eyes and lifted eyebrows answered Ice's question before Nik spoke. "No." Nik reached out and took the stone. His eyes stretched wider and he frowned. "The girl. You said you didn't give it to her."

"Jeni? No. I didn't. What are you saying? She had it—used it?"

"She used it," Nik confirmed, looking thoughtful. "Few have the capability to use medicine stones, even when taught. The first time Jeni dreamed with the stone, I accepted it as a fluke—a coincidental culmination of the right circumstances. But tonight, fully aware of what she had in her possession, she employed the stone intentionally. Apparently her elemental talent is earth-based, and strong; it's no wonder she woke the manitou with a stone statue in her pocket."

Ice had expected Nik to be angry, but his short dissertation was delivered in a worrisome tone that returned the dull ache of dread to Ice's chest. "What?" he asked, his heart beginning to thump harder as the medicine man threw back his covers and swung his feet to the floor. "What's wrong?"

"The stone." Nik opened his closet and pulled out a duffle bag. "It reeks of trouble. When conveying a warning, the stone's desire to alter coming events is powerful, especially when fueled with so much elemental energy. The effect on the dreamer can be quite persuasive."

A bolt of alarm shot through Ice, all his earlier thoughts rushing back. "Oh God, do you think… Jeni…the girl who—" he couldn't finish the thought.

"I don't know what to think," Nik snapped. "Throw my other things in here while I change."

Ice carried out his task, not seeing what he was doing, picturing instead Jeni's earlier frustrated expression; the tears gleaming in her eyes. *I'm supposed to just let you and Nik go after this…this…creature or whatever it is, and put yourselves in harm's way when all this is my fault?* She'd been so determined to help—if she had the same dream again would she have gone after the monster by herself? No, Ice answered the question with renewed anguish, not alone—she took Tyler with her. And Tyler saw Mishebeshu take her.

Nik must've caught the look on Ice's face because he put his hand on his apprentice's shoulder. "Don't assume the worst," he said in a soft voice. "We don't know what the stone showed her, we can't speculate on Jeni's reaction. Do you have a way to contact her?"

Ice frowned at the time display on his phone. "Yeah, I have her number." He hesitated; thumb hovering over her name, as he considered the cottage full of people. There was a good chance he was overreacting.

"It's important, Ice," Nik prodded.

Ice's heart hammered in his chest as he listened to Jeni's phone ring. He lowered the phone from his ear in disappointment. "I got her voicemail." Then he left a quick message for Jeni to call back as soon as possible.

Nik zipped the bag and slung it over his shoulder. "Why don't we head toward the resort? We can confirm she's there and find out what she dreamed. You can try calling her again on the way."

Ice did. Twice. Telling himself there was no reason for concern. With so many people in one cottage, Jeni must be sharing a bedroom, she probably put her phone on vibrate.

But his gut told him something different. The apprehension Nik exuded scared the hell out of Ice. He needed to know Jeni was safe.

"Nik? Can we use the yellow stone—it's a seeking stone, right? Just so we know she's really at the resort?"

"Mmm, it takes too much time. We'd be at the resort long before it could return."

They were still thirty minutes from Rainbow Resort. Ice stared at the road ahead and willed his phone to ring.

"Unless…," Nik said.

"What?" Ice jerked his head toward his passenger.

"Do you have anything of hers? Has she given you anything?"

"Just the statue."

"Anything else? Anything at all. The stone can find a person quickly with something that belongs to them or something given freely—like coins, paper, even a tissue."

Ice shook his head. He'd barely spent any time with Jeni. Even when she gave him her phone number she'd entered it directly into his phone.

He tapped his fingers impatiently on the steering wheel as he waited for a traffic light.

"Pull over," Nik suddenly commanded.

Ice shot a questioning glance at the medicine man and found Nik studying his...arm?...jacket?

"Under the street light," Nik motioned with his hand.

Ice glided up to the curb. "I thought we were in a hurry."

"We are." Nik leaned over and plucked something from Ice's sleeve. He held it up in the light.

It was a long, blonde hair.

✱✱✱

Jeni's knees ached from kneeling on the hard ground. She shifted from one leg to the other, trying to get some relief. At least her head had cleared and Tyler no longer had to hold her up.

"Tyler?"

He grunted.

"I'm sorry about what I said; this isn't your fault."

"I know."

"I was just really scared."

"Interesting reaction."

Jeni carefully considered what she was going to say next. If Tyler hadn't come out here, she'd be by herself and possibly dying right now. The least she could do was explain why she'd yelled at him.

She took a deep breath. "In third grade, there was this boy I was friends with, Randy. We'd been friends since pre-school and he knew I was afraid of the dark. Anyway, one day we were lining up to go to lunch and the teacher asked me to return the basket of reading books to the supply closet upstairs. The basket was kind of cumbersome so she asked Randy to help me. Well, of course we had to get nosey and poke around in the supply closet. I was checking out some Christmas decorations or something when all of a sudden the light went out and the door slammed shut. I called out to Randy and when he didn't answer, I realized he'd done it—shut me in there in the dark."

She paused but Tyler didn't say anything, so she continued. "I ran toward the door, tripped on something and fell. When I made it to the door I couldn't open it. I don't know if it locked from the inside or if it was broken. I yelled for Randy while waving my hands around trying to catch the string to turn the light on. I couldn't find it in the dark. That's when I freaked out."

"I screamed and pounded on the door but the rooms upstairs were only used for special classes, like music or art and the science lab. It was lunch time—no one was around. Eventually I just sat down by the crack of light at the bottom of the door and cried."

"Didn't your teacher wonder what happened to you?"

"She'd left the class in the cafeteria and went to the teacher's lounge to eat her lunch."

"What about your friends?"

"Yeah, eventually they wondered where I was. Still, lunch was our only freedom all day. Not many kids would give that up to go looking for someone. But one girl did. Carolyn. She asked Randy where I was and he must've looked suspicious because she went right to the teacher and told her I never came to lunch."

"Carolyn? The same one I met at Grandpa's funeral?"

Jeni missed a beat, surprised that Tyler remembered her friend, then answered, "Yup, that's her. We've been best friends ever since."

She fell silent, wondering what Tyler might be thinking, then she laughed humorlessly. "You know, telling this now makes it sounds like nothing, but I've never really gotten over my fear of the dark and I'm extremely claustrophobic—put the two together... well, you know. When that door slammed shut over us, I was back in third grade again, and I panicked. I got mad at you to keep from going nuts."

She waited. It was a huge risk; she'd just handed her adversary a buttload of ammo. Ironically, telling Tyler the story had gone against the vow she'd made back then to never trust boys.

"Hate to break it to you, but you qualified for nuts just by roaming around in the woods by yourself in the middle of the night," Tyler said.

There might have been a question there, but Jeni chose to ignore it. Telling Tyler about her fears was hard enough—she couldn't talk to him about her feelings for Ice. Instead she asked a question. "How did you find me?"

"I followed you. When I found your mom's car at the side of the road, you were already out of sight and I wasn't sure which way you went. At first I was going to search the side you parked on, and then I realized the state park was across the road and it seemed a more likely place to start."

"You heard me leave?"

"I'm sleeping on the sofa-bed in the living room, remember?"

"Why did you come after me? Why didn't you tell my mom and dad?"

Tyler took his time answering her question. "I guess I believed you when you said you wouldn't go after the…creature or whatever. Plus, I knew the older guy was still in the hospital." He sighed heavily. "I figured you were just meeting Ice somewhere. If that was the case, once I was sure you were with him, I would've gone back to the cottage."

Jeni was glad Tyler couldn't see her blush. He thought she might be meeting Ice for a midnight rendezvous—the implication there was apparent. She didn't know why it mattered to her, but she didn't want Tyler to think she was that kind of girl.

She cleared her throat. "Uh, just for the record, I wouldn't take my parent's car and drive illegally just to meet a guy."

"Yet." She could hear the smile in his voice.

"There's still time."

Jeni shifted on her knees again. "How much longer can that thing run?"

"Not much longer, I hope."

She couldn't stand to listen to the engine rumbling away above them. She needed distraction. "So you were playing *Breaking Benjamin* in your car today, what other bands do you like?"

That conversation eventually turned into sort of a game where they took turns blurting out as many bands from their iPods as they could remember. Jeni used an alphabetical strategy and had reached 'T' when the motor above coughed and sputtered. They both listened as it hiccupped a few times and then finally stalled.

"Thank God," Jeni sighed.

"Don't move. We'll want the air to clear. Plus we should listen for any signs that someone's still up there."

Jeni listened for noise from above while she continually shifted from knee to knee. She swore the grit had worked its way through her jeans, her skin, and now grated directly on bone. There was no indication their captor remained outside the cellar.

"This is what I think we should do," Tyler said in a low voice. "First, if I can raise the door even a little bit, maybe you can shove something in there so the fumes in here can escape."

"Okay," Jeni agreed.

"Then we can take turns shoveling out that tunnel. Whoever's not shoveling should probably still breathe over here." Tyler began to pull his jacket out of the opening around his face. "Ready?"

"Ready." Jeni gripped her jacket and took a couple of deep breaths.

"Go!"

They attempted to spring into action, their stiff knees preventing an accelerated pace. Jeni groaned but kept moving. She found the branch she'd dropped when she fell. Tyler had the bigger branch and already had the end against the door.

Jeni held the limb horizontally in both hands high above her head. She positioned it at the crack at the edge of the door and leaned forward slightly. "Okay," she squeaked out, trying not to expel her breath.

Tyler heaved and the door lifted slightly. Jeni shoved her stick forward and it jammed into the earth. She let go and it stayed put. She exhaled in a rush and darted for the furnace as she fought the urge to breathe in great gulps of air. Seconds later, Tyler was beside her.

"I think if we try…" Tyler panted, "One more time, you can get that branch in farther."

Jeni nodded.

They both sucked in air and hurried back to their positions. Tyler heaved again and Jeni pushed forward. Her stick didn't move. Trying again, she pushed down on the end of the branch and shoved it upward on an angle. At first it resisted, then broke through the looser surface dirt, sliding through the crack, and propping the door open an inch or so. Tyler dropped his branch and they returned to the furnace, gasping for air.

"I'll shovel first," Tyler said.

The cellar still reeked of fumes and Jeni put her jacket around her head to keep the poisoned gas from invading her breathing space. Without the jacket muffling the sound of metal scraping dirt, she might have missed the rustle and crunch of leaves above until it was too late.

"Tyler!" she hissed.

He paused, then he heard it too. The swishing grew louder, quickly. Tyler carefully lowered the shovel to the ground, tiptoed over to Jeni, and crouched next to her.

There was no doubt someone was up there.

Jeni's heart wanted to explode in her chest. When the crazy guy found out they were still alive, he would find some other way to kill them. Asphyxiation might have been preferable to whatever the psychopath had in store for them now. A small cry of fear escaped from the back of her throat.

Tyler squeezed her shoulder and leaned in, his mouth close to her ear, then they both recoiled from the sound of thumps and scraping on the trap door.

The logs were being removed.

My Creator, let me live today with an open heart.
Let me realize to be vulnerable is a strength,
not a weakness. Let me realize the power of
an open heart. Let me be available to truth. If
I get into trouble, let me hear the whisper of
your guidance. Let me make heart decisions
and let my head catch up on that decision.

—Audrey Shenandoah, Onandaga

CHAPTER 11

Ice looked up from the empty space on the dash where the yellow stone had been a moment earlier. "Should we still drive toward the resort?"

"Might as well. Even if she's not there, we'll be near Lake Itasca."

A cold stab of fear pierced Ice's chest. He didn't want to think about Jeni being anywhere, except safe in her bed.

As if reading his mind, Nik said, "Don't worry, it'll find her fast using her hair. If that was her hair?"

Ice pressed his lips together. He had no appreciation for Nik's attempt to lighten the mood. "It's hers."

The minutes on the Jeep's clock ticked by in slow motion. Ice tried Jeni's phone again. He didn't expect her to answer; it was a way to pass the time. Twelve minutes after the seeking stone disappeared, it reappeared on the dash making Ice jump.

Nik snatched it and held it in his palm, eyes closed.

Ice glanced back and forth from road to Nik. "Well?"

"She's not at the cottage."

Ice's throat closed up.

"She's under…"

"Water?" Ice moaned. "Oh God…"

"Ground," Nik said, squeezing Ice's arm. "She's in some kind of underground area."

"Like a cave?" Ice whispered.

Nik turned his head slowly from side to side, eyes closed. "Perhaps, but the shape seems too well defined." The medicine man sat motionless, employing all of his senses. "There must be a road not too far away…I smell exhaust…and…wood smoke? Also, a prevalent earthy smell—like wet dirt—my guess is the place is probably near water."

"Great," Ice muttered, "that narrows it down." The area had hundreds of lakes. He stopped at an intersection and rubbed his sweaty palms on his jeans. "Left toward the resort or right toward the state park?"

Nik held the stone out to Ice. "Take it."

Ice raised his eyebrows, but accepted the stone.

"You have a connection with Jeni, sense her."

Ice cupped the stone in both hands. Though his heart beat at an accelerated pace, he closed his eyes and tried to clear his head of all thoughts except for Jeni. He sought her essence; her soul.

He had no idea what he was doing.

Setting the stone on the seat next to him, Ice made a right turn. He cruised the highway skirting the east edge of the state park, guided by intuition, nerves humming on overdrive.

He nearly flew past the cars on the side of the road.

Nik pitched forward and then was flung back in his seat as Ice slammed on the brakes. He threw the Jeep into reverse and backed to the cars. "Both of these cars were at the cottage. I think the silver one is Jeni's cousin's." His voice wavered and he swallowed hard. Oh God, she was with Tyler. "Should we…should we find the police down at the lake?"

"Ice." Nik waited until his apprentice met his gaze. "Don't jump to conclusions. Let's check it out here first."

Ice leaned forward, struggling to breathe normally, and retrieved a small flashlight from his glove box. He nodded across the road. Toward Lake Itasca. Nik followed him into the woods and they proceeded silently, tracking a trail of footsteps and broken foliage. Ice noted with dismay the two sizes of footprints.

They came to the park road and crossed, picking up the trail. A few steps from the blacktop Ice heard Nik mutter, "Burial grounds." The medicine man's words made Ice's chest constrict further, and he forced himself onward, his pulse racing.

Wrinkling his nose, Ice glanced at Nik. "Smell that?"

Nik nodded.

Ice frowned. Why did he smell exhaust here, a few yards off the road? As glimpses of the lake appeared through the trees, the gassy smell grew stronger. Then his flashlight glinted off something ahead and he hurried forward. When the shape came into view, Ice slowed to steady the beam and trace the object. Was that a motorcycle? On its side?

He shook his head. That's what he smelled. Someone was screwing around on their dirt bike in the woods and it quit or ran out of gas, so they'd left it behind.

Except it was like five a.m. Ice paused and narrowed his eyes. Why would the fumes still linger in the area?

He stepped into the clearing and flicked his light over the bike and some nearby logs. Something here was not right. He could feel it. Coming closer, he scanned the disturbed ground, the hot ball of dread in his stomach flaring with newfound fuel.

His light stopped on a metal ring. Wet dirt. Not a cave. He met Nik's eyes and without a word, they both rushed to the trap door and shoved the logs covering it out of the way. Ice grasped the ring and flung the heavy door open as though it was made of Styrofoam. A rush of fumes issued from the space below.

He directed his light inside and gasped when the beam revealed two bodies lying lifeless on the cellar floor. His brain worked to reconcile the scene before him with his expectation that Mishebeshu had slain Jeni while Tyler watched helplessly.

"No," he choked the word out.

Nik reached out to grab him, but Ice was already in motion. He dropped into the cellar. "Nonononono," he moaned, falling to his knees.

Though she was on her face and her hair hid her features, Ice knew it was Jeni. His hand shook as he reached to gently roll her over. He pressed his thumb on her wrist, eyes downcast and welling with tears.

"Ice?" she said, pulling her hand away.

Ice's head snapped up and Jeni threw herself into his arms. Over her shoulder he saw Tyler sit up and stare wide-eyed.

Then they all started asking questions at once.

"Save the explanations for later," Nik called down. "Get out of there, it smells terrible!"

Tyler already had his hands on the lip of the hole, and his face lifted to the fresh air. He hoisted himself up and Nik helped haul him over the edge. Ice pulled Jeni up from the ground and lifted her by the waist as she held her hands out to Nik and Tyler, then he clambered up to join them.

"Are you all right?" Ice asked Jeni as they tramped into the trees.

"I am now."

He put his arm around her, fingers curled over her shoulder. She slipped her arm around his waist and he sighed, letting the tension of the past few hours ebb.

"I thought you went after the monster and he got you. Then, I saw you down there and…you were…it looked like you guys were dead."

"That was the plan, we wanted whoever tried to kill us to think he'd succeeded and then Tyler was going to jump him."

"Someone tried to kill you? How did you get in there in the first place?"

Jeni began telling Ice about her second dream, but as they emerged into the clearing next to the road,

Tyler approached anxiously. "It's almost six o'clock. We'd better get back before you're grounded for life."

Jeni looked from Tyler to Ice, face troubled. "My dad gets up early."

✳ ✳ ✳

Jeni shifted impatiently from foot to foot. *Where was he?*

As they'd rushed to their cars, Tyler called out that he'd be a few minutes behind her and to wait for him. He'd followed her until she turned west on 113—he continued south.

As soon as she arrived at the cottage she got out of the car. Better to get caught outside than to get caught driving without permission—or a license for that matter. She fought the urge to pace, afraid to activate the motion sensor light.

Jeni jumped when a bright square appeared on the ground—the bathroom light was on. She prayed whoever it was would do their business and go back to bed.

How long had she been here? Where was Tyler?

The lighted square disappeared. She held her breath, waiting to see if the kitchen light went on. Shadow and light flickered across the outside wall of the cottage. Jeni turned to see headlights bobbing on the resort drive.

"Please be Tyler, please be Tyler," she whispered under her breath.

With no attempt at stealth, Tyler pulled up

and parked, exiting the car with a box in his hands. "Doughnuts," was his reply to her raised eyebrows. He slid the box onto the roof of the car, then hit the lever to hinge his driver seat forward and reached into the back seat.

Jeni frowned and shot a glance at the cottage. "Someone was up—in the bathroom," she warned.

"Score," Tyler said and emerged with a bundle in one hand that he thrust at Jeni and a box of baby wipes in the other. "Put this on. Throw your jacket in my car."

Jeni unfurled a seriously wrinkled sweatshirt. "I don't—"

"We smell like we had front seats at a demolition derby. Now hurry up," he urged, peeling off his own jacket and tossing it into the back seat. Then he held out a baby wipe. "I'll have to thank Josie later for leaving these in my car."

Jeni wriggled out of her jacket. The sweatshirt bore the name of a Wisconsin college, but she supposed that was easier to hide than a smell. Swallowing her reluctance at wearing something that looked as though it'd lived in Tyler's car for months, she pulled the shirt over her head. By the time she'd wiped her face and hands, Tyler stood at the door, doughnuts in hand, and she hurried to join him. He swung the door open and stepped into the kitchen without hesitation. Jeni followed his lead, eyes darting nervously around the empty room. She breathed a sigh of relief.

Tyler slid the box of doughnuts on the table while Jeni kicked her shoes off. Before she could confer with him about their story, though, her dad walked into the room.

"Wow, what're you two doing up?"

Jeni busied herself by digging in her purse for some scented lotion, leaving Tyler to field the question, but when she turned, he was looking at her expectantly. With her back to her father, she gaped at her cousin.

"What?" Tyler returned an angelic gaze. "It was your idea."

"Yeah…uh…" Jeni looked daggers at Tyler then dropped her gaze to the table. "Doughnuts. We went for doughnuts."

"Really," her dad said. "You and Tyler? At six a.m.?"

Jeni rubbed the lotion on her hands and turned only slightly toward her dad, "Well, I couldn't drive by myself," she said, avoiding the real questions.

Tyler lifted the lid on the box of doughnuts. He looked them over and selected a nut-covered cake doughnut. He ate a third of it in one bite. "Fresh," he mumbled around the food in his mouth. "Gotta get them when they're fresh."

"It's vacation dad," Jeni held her hands in front of the writing on the sweatshirt, still rubbing them together. "I figured we gotta have doughnuts."

Jeni's dad turned away, apparently satisfied with the explanation, "I'd better get the coffee going."

Jeni selected a glazed doughnut, quickly set it on a napkin, and then slipped from the room before her dad could press the issue of going for doughnuts at the crack of dawn. She paused in the living room waiting for Tyler to follow. He sauntered in, still chewing the last bite of his doughnut, a glass of milk in his hand.

"You could've let me in on the plan when we were out by your car," she hissed.

"You're welcome for saving your ass."

Jeni closed her mouth on what she wanted to say next. She hated it when he was right. "How do you come up with this stuff anyway?"

"Years of practice," he said, draining his glass of milk and grinning at her. "Take this in the kitchen for me, would ya?" He handed her the empty glass. "I'm going to sleep for a couple hours."

"Sure thing," Jeni said sarcastically, but she took the glass. Peeping around the doorway, she saw her dad at the kitchen table. She set the glass in the sink without a sound and then quickly grabbed a bottle of water from the refrigerator.

Her head throbbed so she stopped in the bathroom for a couple of acetaminophen tablets, which she washed down with half the bottle of water. Careful not to wake her grandma, she tiptoed into her room and set the doughnut on the nightstand. She was far too nauseated to think about eating it.

She slipped out of her filthy jeans, grateful her dad hadn't noticed how dirty they were—her mom certainly would have. Dropping the pants next to her suitcase, she peeled off the sweatshirt and then her exhaust-permeated pajama top and found a clean t-shirt to put on. The night's events whirled in her head as she sank into the pillow. Her body ached for rest and she closed her eyes, though she didn't think she'd be able to sleep.

She was wrong.

Barbara Pietron

✱ ✱ ✱

"Be out in a minute," Jeni yelled through the bathroom door to her aunt. She spit toothpaste into the sink and looked in the mirror. Her hair was still damp but at least it no longer reeked of fumes. She tucked her toothbrush into its travel case and headed for the kitchen.

Ice sat at the table with a cup of coffee, listening to Tyler's mom chatter as she pulled food out of the refrigerator. He smiled when Jeni entered the room. "Hey, I heard you got up early to get doughnuts," he nodded at the box on the table.

"Yup. Want one?" She had to remember to act as if she hadn't seen him since last night.

"Actually, I wondered if you wanted to go out for breakfast."

A chance to talk—alone? "Yeah." Jeni caught her aunt's smile and knew the eagerness in her voice hadn't gone unnoticed. She felt her cheeks flush. "Let me check with my mom."

Jeni found her mom making the bed.

"Hey Mom, is it okay if I go get breakfast with Ice?"

"I thought you got doughnuts?"

"Hours ago," Jeni replied, although she'd devoured her doughnut only forty-five minutes ago when she awoke ravenous. "I need real breakfast."

Her mom straightened and Jeni recognized the 'thinking about it' look on her face. "Well…I guess so. But you realize today is our last day here and I expect you to spend time with the family."

"It's just breakfast, Mom."

"All right then."

As Jeni retrieved her purse she realized this would be their first real "date"—the first time Ice was picking her up and taking her out somewhere.

Too bad it was also the last.

How suckish. She finally met a guy who wasn't an idiot and he lived twenty hours away.

Her pensive mood must've been evident, because Ice paused before starting the Jeep and looked over at her. "Are you okay?"

Jeni nodded. "I just need to eat."

He studied her for a few more seconds then started the car. Once they were on the road, he tried again. "Did something happen? I mean, at first you seemed pretty upbeat—considering the night you must've had—and now it's like the wind has been taken from you sails."

Jeni didn't respond.

Ice reached over, rubbed the top of her leg lightly, and left his hand there.

Jeni sighed, knowing that if they were any other couple, he'd be holding her hand right now. "It's my last day here," she finally said.

"I know," he said quietly. "That's why I came over early."

"Well it's a good thing you did because my mom expects me to spend the rest of the day with the family."

"Oh."

"It's not really fair. They're my relatives, I'll see them again."

Ice glanced at her, eyebrows raised. "You think you won't see me again?"

"I...it was a long drive here...how..." Jeni trailed off, not sure what to say. She didn't want it to be over with Ice. She assumed they might keep in touch for a while but eventually things would just fizzle out because of the distance between them.

They were both quiet for a minute and then Ice spoke, his voice soft and low. "Do you want to?"

"Yeah." Jeni said it with conviction, and peeked through her hair at him. He had to ask?

Ice let his breath out, as if he'd been holding it in. Apparently he hadn't known how she felt. "Me too," he said, the corners of his mouth curling upward.

The diner was a little mom-and-pop place in nearby Lake George. Ice parked and they both released their seat belts. Instead of opening the door though, Ice turned to Jeni. "Hey," he reached to brush her hair back, retaining a lock to twist between his fingers. When she met his eyes he said, "We'll find a way, okay?"

Jeni nodded. Swallowed.

His fingers slid into her hair, cradling the back of her head.

A small table littered with trinkets clouded her vision.

He leaned forward to kiss her. Jeni closed her eyes.

A new image—a trio of lit candles, flames dancing.

It was like trying to watch TV while someone kept changing the channel.

Then Ice kissed her like he was making a promise. He filled up her senses, dispelling the visions.

When he pulled away, Jeni opened her eyes to his hungry gaze. His intent stare fanned the flames he'd already started. "We probably should go eat," her strangled voice forced the words out.

The public venue had a normalizing effect, and when they were seated, Jeni filled Ice in on the second dream.

Ice's eyes widened. "Did you find the statue?"

"No. There was a cloth, but it was empty."

He frowned. "Nik mentioned the statue was wrapped up inside his duffle bag."

"So the statue was there, I was just too late." Jeni's insides turned cold. "So if that dream was true, the first dream is going to happen. Just like I saw."

"Not necessarily. Remember, what you saw is a possible future. It's not predestined."

"So what will you do without the statue? What will change to make tonight different than my first dream?"

Ice didn't reply as a waitress poured coffee for him and set a glass of orange juice in front of Jeni. He used the interruption to change the subject. "What happened at the cellar? And what was Tyler doing there?"

The aroma of bacon and hash browns hung heavily in the small diner, and Jeni's stomach growled. She intermittently examined the menu as she recounted the crazy mishaps of the previous night, leaving out Tyler's thought that she might be out for a rendez-vous with Ice.

"So someone tried to kill you."

Jeni's eyes rose from the menu to meet Ice's. "Absolutely."

"Presumably the same person who stole the statue." Ice glowered into his coffee cup.

"It's the only thing that makes sense." She took a long drink of her orange juice, guessing that, at this point, the dull throb at the base of her skull was more due to low blood sugar than breathing fumes in the cellar.

Ice scanned his menu, frowning. "Nik's puzzled about this human minion. It's not how the underwater manitou operates. He tricks people into serving him, not killing for him—he prefers to do that himself."

"How did you guys find us anyway?" Jeni spied the waitress heading their way as Ice began to explain. Once their food was ordered, she picked up the conversation thread. "Seriously? You found me by using a piece of my hair? From your jacket?"

Ice nodded and chuckled.

"I guess I should give you something so you can always find me." Jeni grinned.

"Oh. That reminds me," Ice reached into a jacket pocket and handed Jeni a small brown bag, "I got this for you."

Jeni withdrew a bundle of tissue and unfolded it to reveal a necklace or pendant of sorts—a painted stone laced through with a soft piece of hide. The top half of the stone depicted a blue sky and green forest. The bottom appeared to be grey boulders lining black water. In the center was the face of a beautiful Indian girl.

"Itasca," Ice explained. "The world above and the underworld. It reminded me of the day we met."

"It's perfect." Jeni smiled up at him. She thought she noticed a blush surfacing on his cheeks, although his tan skin made it hard to say for sure. Sliding from the booth, she perched on the edge of Ice's bench with her back to him and passed the necklace over her shoulder. "Put it on for me?"

"I chose stone because Nik said it's your elemental source of strength." He finished tying the knot and when he lifted her hair over it, Jeni shivered. "I wanted you to have a souvenir of your time here, since the one you bought has disappeared."

Jeni fingered the stone, and smiled shyly, touched by Ice's gesture. She returned to her side of the booth just as the waitress arrived with their food. She dug into her food as soon as the waitress turned away. A few bites later, a thought occurred. "Ice, you explained how you found us, but why were you looking? How did you know we were in trouble?"

He looked up from his plate. "The dream stone. Nik sensed trouble and he knew you used it."

"And he called you in the middle of the night to come get him from the hospital?"

"Not exactly," Ice paused, an odd look on his face.

"What are you not telling me? Is Nik even madder at me now?"

Ice shook his head and regarded her warily. "We got a report that a girl went missing last night. The boy with her said a monster took her." His eyes fell to his plate where he aimlessly pushed his scrambled eggs around. "When Nik said you were in trouble…" he looked up at her, "…I thought it was you."

Jeni's eyebrows shot up. "You thought I went after the monster?" She snorted in disbelief. "Ice, I'd have no idea what to do if…" she let the comment die, choosing not to put the unthinkable scenarios into words.

Ice's lips curled in a playful smile. "You sounded ready to go to war yesterday."

"I still am," Jeni retorted, her face serious. "Maybe if Nik would've let me do something, that girl would be alive right now. And while we're on the subject, you never answered my question. What are you guys going to do without the statue?"

She picked up a piece of bacon and watched him expectantly. He made a small project out of selecting a jelly and then spreading it on his toast. "You said something has to be done, Nik must have some idea," she prompted. He wasn't going to get away with changing the subject again.

Finally Ice lifted his eyes to hers and Jeni glimpsed his internal struggle. He opened his mouth, closed it, and took a bite of his toast.

"What?" Jeni's mind raced, trying to figure out what Ice didn't want to say. Suddenly, it stuck her. "You need me," she whispered.

The immediate widening of his eyes gave away the truth even though Ice shook his head. "No, I told Nik no," he muttered.

"No to what?"

Ice dropped his toast, pressed his hand to his forehead for a moment and then swiped his fingers through his hair. He scanned the diner, his gaze eventually returning to Jeni. "I told him I wouldn't ask you. Not after yesterday."

"I thought you had to do whatever he said," she shot back and watched as Ice's mouth twitched up at the corners. Good. He'd caught the irony she was going for. "So he changed his mind about me after the statue was stolen?" Jeni ate a bite of hash browns.

"Not exactly. After you and Tyler left this morning, Nik and I went back over any clues we'd received from the spirit world and he came to the conclusion that you should be there."

Jeni swallowed and her mouth dropped open. "What kind of clues?"

Ice retrieved his toast and consumed a mouthful of eggs while considering his answer. "To start with, I dreamed about you—after we met that first day." After telling her about his dream he recounted Nik's vision quest. "In my dream an owl warned me to get out of the water. Nik realized the bird that sent the lightning bolts in his vision was also an owl. He thinks the owl represents you."

"So…what? Are you saying I can shoot lightning bolts?"

Ice smiled. "No. When lightning strikes a beach, the sand melts into a fragile tubular stone. We call it a thunderstone. Remember I told you about the Thunderers?"

"Sure, the spirits that fight the underwater monster."

"Right. Thunderstones are a gift from the Thunderers. Nik thinks his vision revealed a way for us to influence the underwater monster—even without the statue." Ice hesitated. He fiddled with the handle of his coffee mug then lowered his voice and continued. "He thinks a thunderstone in your hands would be powerful medicine."

Jeni blinked as conflicting emotions barraged her all at once: surprise, vindication, disbelief, and ultimately, fear. "Nik thinks *I* can control the monster with a thunderstone?"

Ice set his fork down and sat back. "Basically—yeah. You've shown an aptitude for stone—first the statue and then the dream stone."

"My…what did you call it? Elemental source of power?"

Ice nodded. "In Nik's vision, an owl bestowed the gift…" he shook his head again. "No, I won't try to talk you into it. It's way too dangerous. You already almost got killed over this whole thing."

Jeni also sat back and contemplated Ice across the table. She ignored the trepidation wending its way through her midsection. "I still feel the same way I did yesterday about making this right," she said evenly. *Plus, I can't let my premonition come true*, she told herself. Then, draining her glass of orange juice, she clunked it down on the table. "I'm in."

"Even after last night?"

"Especially after last night. Someone tried to kill Tyler and me. Other people have died already. Let's end it."

Ice's look of part wonder and part admiration helped smother her growing apprehension. "I've never known a girl like you." He didn't seem to be aware that he'd spoken out loud.

On the way back to the cottage, Ice informed Jeni that Nik was meeting with the elders to confer on their best course of action, and he'd call her later with details: where, when, and how.

Jeni didn't say anything, but her thoughts returned to her mom wanting her to spend time with the family today.

She hoped that didn't include tonight.

Knowledge is a beautiful thing, but the using of knowledge in a good way is what makes for wisdom. Learning how to use knowledge in a sacred manner, that's wisdom to me. And to me, that's what a true Elder is.

—Sun Bear, Chippewa

CHAPTER 12

W hat do you mean we have to find a thunderstone?" Ice practically shouted, knowing they were alone in the house. "I thought you already had a couple."

Nik's face remained calm. "I do have thunderstones. We need *the* thunderstone. The one sent by the thunderbird in my vision."

"You realize we have hours, Nik, not days?" Ice paced the length of the living room, which meant he took four steps and then turned.

"I think you can do it."

"Wait a minute—when did *we* turn into *me?*"

"Think about it Ice, I'm meeting with the elders, I can't be in two places at the same time." Nik was the picture of serenity in the easy chair, only his eyes moved, tracking his apprentice.

"And I don't have any medicine stones, remember?" Ice had never been this disrespectful with

Nik—but he'd never been this stressed out either. "I barely even know how to use them."

"Medicine stones weren't the method I had in mind. I can describe the scene for you."

Ice snorted in disbelief. "Minnesota: The Land of Ten Thousand Lakes! You're talking about finding a needle in a haystack."

"Don't sell yourself short Ice, you have talents that I don't. Talents which give you a tool better suited for this task than a medicine stone."

Ice stopped moving and glanced over at Nik. "What talents? What tool?"

"Technology. You're good with computers. I can tell you in detail all the things I saw in my vision that may help identify the lake. You'll probably find it faster than my medicine stone would."

"How do we even know where to begin looking?"

"The things we see in visions are relevant to the guidance we seek. The lake must be in the area, maybe even on the reservation; if not, it'll be close."

Ice didn't realize how worked up he was until his heart rate slowed while he thought over Nik's idea. He was good at doing research on the Internet. And if Nik was certain of the area, it narrowed the search considerably. He took a deep breath. "Okay, tell me the details."

Nik went over the vision twice and answered Ice's questions, when possible, before he had to leave for the tribal council office. "I'll call when the meeting's over."

Ice nodded.

Nik locked eyes with his apprentice. "Your

training may not be complete, but make no doubt about it—you are a medicine man. Be confident in your talents and don't forget that symbolism and dual meanings are everything in our business. Don't let facts get in the way of your intuition."

Ice closed the door behind him and watched through the glass as Nik walked to his truck. Nik stopped, turned around, and said something. Ice didn't hear him, but he read Nik's lips, "Good luck."

"I'm sure I'll need it," he muttered on the way to his room. Ice knew once he started surfing the Internet, it would be easy to lose track of all the thoughts floating around in his head. So as his computer booted up, he wrote down everything Nik told him that he thought would help in the search.

He'd start with satellite maps. In the vision, Nik had left the forest for open farmland, so Ice typed in Chippewa National Forest. The full-page map didn't show the borders of the national forest, although the little navigation map in the corner did, and Ice slowly moved his search box to follow the perimeter of the green shaded area. He continually zoomed in and out on the satellite image to search for farmland bordering a lake.

As he'd suspected, he found many.

Ice dug through a stack on the table which served as his makeshift desk, and pulled out a lined pad. He wrote all the criteria the lake should meet across the top of the page: shape, size, and amount of surrounding forest or farmland. Looking back at the computer screen, each time he came across a possibility, he wrote down the name of the lake and checked off the features he could see from the satellite map.

Since the images became grainy and blurry the closer he zoomed in on them, he knew the search would involve some footwork. He ran out to his Jeep and retrieved a county map so he could mark each lake listed as a possibility.

He worked meticulously for hours, knowing there wouldn't be time for a second attempt. The thunderstone must go with them tonight.

When the search box had gone full-circle, landing back at his starting point, the list was two and a half pages long. He scanned it, circling entries that had all four criteria checked. He'd go to those first.

He stopped in the kitchen to grab a pop for the road and was astonished to see it was after two o'clock. His stomach grumbled, reminding him he hadn't eaten since breakfast. He downed two pieces of ham while he stood in front of the refrigerator and grabbed an apple to go.

He was running out of time.

✳ ✳ ✳

For the third time that week, Jeni followed the path leading to the Mississippi Headwaters. Though surrounded by family, she walked alone with her thoughts. The occasional breaks of sun through the clouds had grown less frequent as the day went on, and the gloominess seemed to match her mood.

Last day of vacation blues.

But it was more than that, wasn't it? It was hard

to believe how much had changed in only a few days. She'd come here thinking she knew who she was and her relative place in life.

Now all of that had been turned upside down. Did her newfound talent have anything to do with her great-grandma's comment about her family's ancestry? Or was she putting the two things together because she learned about them at the same time? In either case, Jeni fully intended to do some research when she got home. Not because she wanted to exercise any innate power she might have, but rather to avoid releasing it by accident and causing destruction.

And death.

Again.

At least two people had died here and despite Ice's protests, Jeni still felt at fault. Although she was terrified about what might happen tonight, she was determined to fix what she'd screwed up.

She sighed.

On top of everything else, she'd met Ice and opened a door on all kinds of crazy new feelings. As unlikely and unexpected as it was, she'd completely fallen for him.

Jeni's prior experience with kissing was not only scarce but more about enduring them than enjoying them. Kissing Ice was like leaving the planet and floating in space. Just thinking about it started a warm sensation in her chest that radiated throughout her body.

She shook her head to clear her thoughts and followed the others onto the bridge where they'd scattered the ashes.

She needed a plan.

Jeni knew better than to just ask if she could go out with Ice tonight. Something special would have to be happening. A chance of a lifetime sort of thing.

Unfortunately she sucked at lying—as evidenced by the day she talked Tyler into driving her to the hospital—and the doughnut thing.

She ambled up the dead end path that led to the opposite side of the headwaters. There was Tyler—standing on the outcropping at the line of boulders with his dad and her dad, the wind making their hair stand up. No doubt they would eventually walk across.

Jeni took a step back, but she'd already been spotted.

"Hey kiddo," her dad greeted her. "We're considering making the crossing. Want to join us?"

Jeni made a face. "No thanks, just here for the view." She was relieved when one of her aunts stepped up next to her.

"Hey Jeni. Has Ice ever mentioned if they do any demonstrations at the reservation?"

"Demonstrations?"

"Like tribal dances or ceremonies, stuff like that."

"Mmm." *Dingdingdingdingding.* A little alarm went off in Jeni's head. "He's never mentioned anything about public demonstrations." Her mind was working overtime to put the idea together. "I know he's got something going on tonight, but I didn't get the impression that it was public."

Jeni's aunt pointed. "Check it out, there goes your dad."

"I gotta get a picture of this." Jeni pulled her

camera out of her purse.

The distraction allowed her some time to work out a plausible scenario in her head. After snapping a few photos, she found her mom.

"Check it out." Jeni stood close so her mom could view the back of the camera and then tabbed through the pictures she'd just taken.

"Men," Jeni's mom shook her head, laughing. "They never stop being boys."

As they headed to meet others on the trail, Jeni asked, "So, Mom, what are we doing later tonight?"

"I'm not sure what everyone's thinking. Any ideas?"

"Well...there's some kind of tribal ceremony tonight that Ice invited me to. I thought it would be a unique opportunity." Jeni chose her words carefully. "You know, experience Native American culture."

"Huh. That does sound interesting, but I thought we'd all want to do something together. Maybe a card game or something?"

"Oh."

Jeni's hopes sank.

❋ ❋ ❋

Ice's Jeep was parked on the side of a road that ran between two lakes. He climbed inside, picked up his list, and drew a line through Dark Lake and Clear Lake. Sighing, he drove toward Highway 71. Next stop, Battle Lake, near Northome.

He glanced at the clock on his radio. Crap. He'd

been at this for nearly three hours and only covered a quarter of the area—a third at best. The more lakes he looked at, the less confident he was about the search. Everything looked so different on the ground compared to the satellite photos. In the interest of time he'd decided to look only at the lakes that met all of the criteria—now he wondered at the wisdom of that assumption.

As he turned onto the county road that would get him close to Battle Lake, he checked the list to see what was next. Medicine Lake, over by Blackduck. He craned his neck to see across the fields, his vision hampered by the darkening skies. It appeared there was no easy access to this lake.

He could not catch a break today.

Thankful for his Jeep, he guided the four-wheel-drive vehicle down a dirt road that was little more than two ruts between a farmer's fields. The bumpy ride provided the most direct route toward the lake. As the view of the water opened in front of him, he knew immediately it wasn't right. Slowing, he bounced the Jeep over the ruts to turn around.

He groaned when his cell phone rang and rested his foot on the brake as he dug the phone from his pocket.

"Hey Jeni." He released the brake and let the vehicle roll forward.

"Ice. Finally. I've been trying to reach you for a few hours. I have some bad news. My mom wants me to stay here tonight." Every word rang with frustration. "Do you know when Nik wants to do this? Maybe I can sneak out."

"No, don't do that. Don't worry about it." He tried to sound soothing—to mask his disappointment. "It doesn't look like I'm going to find the thunderstone anyway."

"You're looking for a thunderstone? I guess I thought Nik already had one."

Ice sighed, his earlier exasperation returning. "Oh, he does. But he wants this one. The one the owl sent in his vision."

"But how could you possibly—"

"Don't ask," Ice interrupted. "I'll explain later."

A silence stretched out and he knew what she was going to say next.

"You won't go will you? If you don't find the stone?"

"I guess I should call Nik. Maybe he'll wait until we can be more prepared. Without you or the thunderstone I don't know what will happen." What he meant was he didn't know what Nik might decide, but Jeni took his words literally.

"I do. I know what'll happen."

"Jeni, that's not wh—"

She wasn't listening to him.

"Please," she pleaded. "Please don't go. Please Ice..." He could hear the threat of tears in her voice.

"Hey... hey Jeni, let me call Nik, okay? Don't get upset. We don't know what he'll decide. And I might find the thunderstone after all."

No reply.

"Jeni?"

"Yeah."

"I'll talk to Nik and call you back, okay?"

"Okay."

Ice pulled out on the highway, en route to the next lake. While he was in an area with cell service he ought to see if he could reach Nik at the tribal council office. Even if the meeting of elders was still in session, Nik would be notified of a call from his apprentice.

"Ice, how's the search going?"

"Not so well. No luck yet.

"Have faith Ice. I do."

"There's something else Nik. I just spoke to Jeni; she can't make it." Ice paused and when Nik didn't say anything, he continued. "Do you think maybe we should wait? We can get together the medicine men from nearby reservations...we'll have more time to plan and to find this thunderstone."

"No, keep looking, we have an advantage tonight. Warriors far more fearsome than medicine men will join us. The elders are watching Doppler radar."

Ice opened his mouth but before any sound came out, Nik continued.

"There's a whopper of a thunderstorm heading our way."

***

By dinnertime, a layer of clouds obscured the sky and the air outside had taken on the sickly, greenish orange that preludes a large storm cell. Every now and then lightning lit the distant horizon. Jeni hardly noticed any of this, wondering if Ice found the thunderstone and if Nik would hold off if they didn't have it.

She pushed food around on her plate, deciding to call Ice as soon as she was free from dinner. Relieved when everyone scattered after the meal, she hurried to the sink with her dishes, then turned and collided with her aunt.

"Whoa! Sorry Jeni, didn't mean to sneak up behind you."

"It's okay." Jeni moved to step away.

"Hang on; I came to tell you something. We were talking about what everyone was doing tonight and your mom said Ice invited you to a tribal function—the one you mentioned earlier?"

"Yeah, she already told me I couldn't go."

"I know, but it looks like there's more than one plan tonight—everyone had different ideas about what they wanted to do. So I asked your mom if I could take you to the ceremony. I admit it was partly selfish because I'd really like to go, but she said it was okay!"

Speechless at first, Jeni tried to process the ramifications of this new development. "Wow…really?"

"Yup." Her aunt squeezed Jeni's arm and grinned.

"I…uh…I have to call Ice," Jeni said, reaching for her phone. "I already told him I couldn't go."

"Well…tell him now you can. Get directions too."

Uh-oh. Her plan backfired big-time. How was she going to get out of this?

Jeni pressed send as she headed across the lawn.

"Jeni! I—ying—all you."

"Ice, you're breaking up."

"—eather. Jen—"

Then he was gone.

Frantically, she tried the call again while rushing to the end of the dock, hoping for better reception. With her back to the gusting wind, she cupped a hand over her mouth and phone.

Wind noise wasn't an issue. The call didn't go through.

Just fabulous! Jeni shoved the phone in her pocket and wrapped her arms around herself. Though it was chilly, she needed a few minutes to think before she went back inside and talked to her aunt.

Duh! She didn't even have to lie. She'd simply tell her aunt she couldn't get Ice on the phone, there would be no details—no destination, no time, no directions.

Unfortunately, it didn't work.

"You know what?" Jeni's aunt said in reply. "A group is heading to the casino. Let's just go with them. Someone there is bound to know about this ceremony or will at least point us in the right direction. Besides, maybe as we head that way you'll be able to reach Ice."

In a last lame effort, Jeni found her mom washing dishes. She picked up a towel and began drying them. "So, no card game huh?"

"Nope, it looks like everyone has their own plans."

"You know, I haven't been able to reach Ice and I would feel bad if Aunt Jessie drove me all the way to the reservation for nothing."

"Well, she's excited about it so you might as well go and see what you can find out."

"I guess."

"Earlier you sounded like this was important to

you; I thought you'd be happy about Jessie taking you out there." Jeni's mom studied her intently. "Is there a reason you don't want to go with your aunt?"

Jeni blushed. *Yes, but not the reason you're thinking.* "It's not that Mom, I was just trying to be considerate."

She turned away with a bowl in her hand and nearly dropped it when she saw Tyler picking up a map from the kitchen table. He was watching her, and when their eyes met, he gave her a hard stare and raised one eyebrow. He'd obviously heard their conversation.

Now she'd have to avoid him or he would grill her about what she was up to.

Fantastic. This night just keeps getting better and better.

*When you carry the medicine, some-
times you have to carry it a long way.*

—Buffy Sainte-Marie, Cree

CHAPTER 13

Six family members in two cars headed for the casino; Jake and Josie rode with Tyler, in his car, and Jeni and two of her aunts in the other car. The good news—Jeni had eluded conversation with Tyler. The bad news—she had about forty-five minutes to figure out what to do when they got there.

The black skies defied the orange readout of 7:22 glowing from the car's dash. Marsh grasses whipped in the wind on either side of the road while lightning put on a show on the western horizon.

No rain yet.

The tension of the coming storm weighed heavily on Jeni's chest. Or was it just her nerves?

She ran various scenarios through her mind. Once they arrived at the casino, she'd somehow split from the group. Then she'd return with the news that…the ceremony was private—or even better—cancelled.

About halfway to their destination her aunt asked if she wanted to try Ice again. Jeni got out her phone, thinking about what she would say to him if he actually did answer.

She pressed send.

After a brief burst of static, the call dropped.

She had an idea.

"Ice? Oh, I'm so glad I got through, I've been trying you for hours."

Jeni listened to dead space for a few seconds.

"Mmm. The weather—that's what I figured, too. So guess what? My aunt is giving me a ride out to the reservation."

Pause.

"Yeah, we're on our way to the casino now. Where is this thing going to be? Is it nearby?"

Jeni was almost glad she hadn't reached Ice. She imagined how confused he would be.

"All right, great. That'll be a lot easier. Okay, see you there."

Jeni's aunt craned her neck to see Jeni in the rear view mirror. "No directions?"

"Just keep following Tyler. Ice said he'll meet us at the casino."

Okay, she'd bought herself a way to separate from the group. Then what? Time was ticking away and she wasn't sure what her next move should be.

Jeni supposed some people would find her situation exhilarating. They were freaks. She was not a fly-by-the-seat-of-your-pants kind of girl. She wanted a map, a plan; at the very least—an idea.

She had nothing.

∗ ∗ ∗

Ice looked at his watch in despair. He wasn't going to find the stone today. This "shot in the dark" search had become literally just that due to the premature darkness. He had to get much closer to the lakes, which most of the time meant getting out and walking to the shoreline.

He jumped in his Jeep and yanked the door from the wind's grasp, slamming it closed. As soon as the engine was running, he shifted into drive. As he bumped over the access road to Lester Lake, he considered his options.

What he would like to do was call it a day, give up, and go spend time with Jeni before she left tomorrow. Unfortunately, that wasn't one of his choices. He was a medicine man, like Nik said; he had responsibilities.

With a grim smile, Ice admitted it had felt good when Nik told him outright that he was a medicine man.

Suddenly he slammed on the brakes, raising a brown cloud of dust that the wind stole immediately. He snatched the list off the seat next to him and clicked on the map light. "Symbolism and dual meanings," Ice muttered scanning the pages.

Don't let the facts get in the way of your intuition.

That's where he went wrong!

He'd scribbled down all the data and then took off without pausing to look at it with the eye of a medicine man. Ice took a deep breath and slowly released it. His hand crept to his forehead, combing the hair away from his face as he read each lake name. He ignored the circles and the criteria, simply turning the names over in his mind. Near the bottom of the second page, a name nearly jumped off the paper at him.

How did he not notice when he wrote it down in the first place?

Owl Lake.

Ice spread out the county map on the steering wheel and located Owl Lake. It was at least thirty minutes south—the wrong direction.

With his cell phone continually losing a signal, he'd had no luck reaching Jeni or the tribal council office; which meant he didn't know when or where to meet Nik. He could make some educated guesses though. All the deaths had occurred in the same general area. And as for time—Ice leaned forward and looked through the windshield at the sky—the storm would determine that.

If he drove west right now, he could be at the State Park in half an hour and be certain to rendezvous with the storm. If he went to Owl Lake first, it would easily be over an hour before he met up with Nik. He might miss the storm, plus there was no guarantee he would find the thunderstone at Owl Lake.

Ice didn't know what to do. Both choices included risk.

He sat back and closed his eyes. Clearing his mind, he consulted his heart.

A minute later, he was on Route 64, hoping he'd chosen wisely.

✷ ✷ ✷

Since Jeni had never been in a casino, she recoiled from the cacophony of voices, bells, and ratcheting slot machines that greeted her when she stepped inside. Her heart pounded up high in her throat, the way it did when she had to talk in front of a group. Knowing her voice would waver when she spoke, she hoped the noise of the casino would cover for her.

"Okay, I'll go find Ice, you guys wait here." She took off before anyone could protest and lost herself in the crowds.

Once out of sight, Jeni scanned the surroundings to determine the best place to find someone who might be able to help her. She'd already decided to go with the story that the "tribal event" had been cancelled. But while she was here she wanted to find out what she could about Nik and Ice.

At the back of the room Jeni spied a hulk of a man standing in front of a door. He wore the *Men in Black* uniform—a well-tailored suit and dark sunglasses. Her knees turned to Jell-O and she compelled one foot to move in front of the other.

"Excuse me sir." He didn't even glance down at her. "I'm looking for Nik…ah…" Jeni still didn't know either Nik or Ice's last name.

"Whoever you're looking for is not inside." The guy still didn't look at her.

She tried again. "I'm looking for the medicine man, Nik. I don't expect him to be here—I just thought someone here might help me find him."

Something she said got his attention. "How do

you know Nik?"

"I'm a friend of his apprentice, Ice. That's who I need to talk to Nik about."

She thought she saw the corners of the guy's mouth twitch into a semblance of a smile as he eyeballed her from head to toe. His scrutiny totally creeped her out.

Without another word the man produced a ring of keys and turned to unlock the door. Pulling it open, he motioned her into a corridor and stepped in behind her. The definitive snap as the door latched in the quiet hallway caused Jeni to jump. Her stomach churned uncomfortably and she wondered if she'd just made a big mistake.

"Follow me." The man took about three strides and opened a door on his right.

Jeni reluctantly trailed after him.

He flipped on a light and ushered her inside an office. The room contained only bare bones of a business space—a desk, phone, two file cabinets, and a mostly empty bulletin board—no personal pictures and no computer. She stepped to the side warily, staying close to the door. Her instincts screamed that this was a bad situation.

He took off his glasses and eyeballed her. "Friend of Ice, you said?"

Not trusting her voice, Jeni nodded.

"Lucky bastard," he muttered rounding the desk. He picked up the phone receiver and punched a button, his eyes trained on Jeni. "Hey, it's Derek. Is Nik around?"

Jeni looked away uncomfortably and pretended

to study the bulletin board.

"He left the council office a little while ago." The man said, phone still on his ear. "Did you have a message for him or something?"

Jeni started to shake her head then stopped. "Is Ice there or did he leave a message?"

The guy—Derek—rolled his eyes. "Look, I've got better things to do than track down your boyfriend."

"No, no, that's not it at all. Please, it's important."

"What about Ice," he barked into the phone. "Yeah, the apprentice. Right." He hung up the phone. "Nik left a message for Ice."

"What...what was it?"

Derek stepped around the desk and Jeni scooted toward the doorway. "Maybe you could give me a reason to tell you."

Jeni didn't like the way he stressed the word "give" or the way his eyes traveled over her. "I'm a priestess," she blurted out.

He laughed. "Are you now?"

"Yes." She did her best to keep her voice steady. "Please, people have already died. I need to help Nik and Ice..." Jeni backed into the hallway, her heart thrumming like a cornered mouse.

In two long steps Derek was in front of her, his left hand pressed to the wall next to her shoulder, blocking her escape to the casino. "The message," he said softly, "is short." He brought his head alongside hers.

Jeni pressed into the wall behind her and turned her head away. She could hear him breathing in deeply through his nose.

"It said, boat launch, ISP," he whispered. "Now, I just did you a favor…"

Did he think he was persuading her…? Jeni shuddered at the feel of his warm, moist breath on her neck.

Then it was gone.

She saw him reach to his hip with his right hand.

Jeni ducked under his arm and ran for the door. Heart racing, she fumbled with the handle. Before she could open it, Derek was behind her. He reached around her, slid a key into the lock, and pushed the door open.

She glanced up at him and saw he was holding a two-way radio. He poked the keypad without looking at her.

She fled.

Jeni hardly noticed the crowds and slot machines as she wove her way back to the entrance. She no longer cared about the ruse she'd been weaving. Or Derek. Nik's message for Ice had evoked all the images from her premonition.

They're going after it tonight. Alone. It'll happen just like I dreamed.

Jeni's aunt Jessie stood at the service desk. She heard her aunt ask about a tribal ceremony. The woman behind the desk frowned and shook her head.

Jeni drifted over, her mind in a fog.

Jeni's aunt spied her. "Where's Ice? No one seems to know anything about this ceremony."

Before Jeni could respond, a voice spoke up behind her. "That's because it's not a ceremony—it's a teen thing—some kind of social event."

Jeni turned, eyes wide.

Tyler?

"Did you find Ice?" he asked Jeni, one eyebrow arched high on his forehead.

"No. He must not be here yet." She narrowed her eyes, wondering what his angle was.

"Well, the…*event*…is for teens and young adults, so call Ice and tell him I'll drive you there." He stared hard at Jeni then turned to their aunt. "I wouldn't mind meeting some hot Indian girls." He grinned. "I guess that means you're stuck here gambling."

"Sorry Aunt Jessie, I didn't know…" Jeni stammered.

"It's all right Jeni, go and have a good time." Her aunt smiled reassuringly.

Tyler looked around. "I'll let Jake and Josie know they're riding back with you," he said to his aunt.

Jeni stood there numb with disbelief until Tyler returned and grabbed her by the elbow, "Let's go."

Will you ever begin to understand the meaning of the very soil beneath your feet?
From a grain of sand to a great mountain, all is sacred.
Yesterday and tomorrow exist eternally upon this continent.
We natives are guardians of this sacred place.

—Peter Blue Cloud, Mohawk

CHAPTER 14

Y ou're a lousy liar," Tyler said as they weaved through the parking lot.

"Excuse me if I haven't made honing that skill a priority," Jeni spat back at him.

When they reached his car, Tyler opened the driver's side door but Jeni stood with her arms crossed over her chest. "Where are we going?"

"Get in."

A gust of wind blew Jeni's hair across her face and she tossed her head so she could see her cousin. She knew her only choice was to go with Tyler; still she wanted him to know he couldn't push her around. "Tell me where we're going."

"Can we at least talk in the car instead of shouting over the wind?"

"Fine." Jeni yanked the door open and climbed inside. She wasn't sure why she was so furious. Hadn't

Tyler just gotten her out of a major jam?

He plugged the key into the ignition but didn't start the car. "You want to tell me what's going on?"

"Do you want to know? Think about it before you answer, Tyler."

The problem was he already knew too much. And he was in a position to either help or hinder—a situation Jeni found excruciatingly frustrating.

Tyler let his head drop back on the headrest with an exaggerated exhale. "Just tell me."

Jeni relayed her conversation with Ice over breakfast that morning. No beating around the bush; no sugar coating. There wasn't time for games.

"And here I thought that after you ALMOST DIED you'd leave this alone," Tyler said.

"You don't get it, do you? Once I was marked for…elimination, I became a part of this. Whoever tried to kill us knew I was there for the statue. If I'm a threat to this monster, then I have a responsibility to help fight it." Jeni's eyes welled with conviction. She looked out the side window.

Tyler sighed. "Where?"

"The boat launch at Itasca State Park."

They drove west, intermittent lightning exposing the gray skies. Heavy, dark clouds rolled in and packed together like spectators for a sporting event.

Jeni noticed Tyler's left leg jiggling when he wasn't shifting gears. He reached and turned on the stereo, letting the CD that was loaded play, but kept the volume low. "So what do you know about this supposed monster?"

She thought back to the day Ice told her about the

being her statue represented. It seemed so long ago. "They call it a manitou, or spirit; a being of power. Ice said it was…uh…not inhuman…other-than-human I think is how he described it. They call it the underwater lynx. You remember what my statue looked like?" Tyler nodded and she continued. "It's an enormous feline monster with horns and scales."

Jeni shivered. "In my dream, it looked like a huge lizard or a dragon maybe."

Tyler grunted.

"I guess a long time ago some of the medicine men would seek its help, even though it was a dangerous thing to do. In one of the stories Ice told me, the monster asked for the medicine man's son as payment for his help. The guy became a great medicine man but he lost all his sons and his wife."

"So it's greedy and devious," Tyler said.

"Definitely."

"And the theory is the monster tricked a guy into going after us?"

"I guess so. Ice said in most of the stories the manitou tricks people so he can kill them—not so they can do his dirty work. But then, he'd never been imprisoned before."

There was no further conversation; each of them lost in their own thoughts. Like Stormchasers, they raced into the heart of the fury, rolling into the parking area of the boat launch thirty minutes later. A single truck was parked in the lot. Jeni's heart sank as soon as she saw it—it was a pick-up truck. Ice wasn't here.

Tyler pulled up next to the truck and Jeni recognized Nik inside. When the medicine man rolled down his window, she did the same.

"I thought you weren't coming?" The look of surprise was out of place on the medicine man's face.

Jeni rolled her eyes. "It's kind of a long story. Have you heard from Ice?"

"Not for a long time. You?"

She shook her head. "No signal."

Lightning flashed, followed by distant thunder. Nik looked into the sky. "It's good you're here. We can't wait much longer." His eyes flicked to Tyler for a second. "Cousin, right?"

Jeni nodded.

"Why don't you get in so we can talk?"

Jeni closed the window. "You can go back to the casino if you want," she told Tyler. "I'm sure I'll be fine with Nik."

Tyler just shook his head with a smile that held little amusement. "No, I can't. Not only are we supposed to be together at some event but, once again, I'm responsible for you." He opened his door. "Besides, it looks like you're a man down."

Jeni shook her head as she watched Tyler climb into the passenger side of the pick-up truck. She would never understand her cousin. If Nik was surprised by Tyler's presence, he didn't show it. Once Jeni plopped down in the backseat, the medicine man began speaking without preamble.

"This site was chosen to imprison the manitou because it's on sacred land. Located here are burial mounds built over eight hundred years ago by ancestors of American Indians, perhaps even my own ancestors. It's well-known among my people that at sacred sites the membrane between the real world and the spirit world is stretched thin. This is why the guardians were able to protect our people even after death."

"How did the manitou get past the guards?" Jeni asked.

"Two nights ago I found the cave. Before I was knocked out, I saw the remains of the guardians. Their bones were smashed and scattered in the cave; the barrier that protected them destroyed. I didn't understand why the wards failed after all this time.

"When we found you in the cellar and you told of the attempt on your lives, it was clear that there was human involvement. The elders think once the manitou awakened, it was able to find a soul willing to serve it. Since the wards would only affect a spirit, this human could destroy the barrier and the guardians, allowing the creature to escape."

"So this guy is probably still lurking out here somewhere," Tyler stated.

"Right. As long as there's a threat to the manitou's continued freedom, he requires human assistance." Nik didn't look at her, but his statement backed up what Jeni had said in the casino parking lot: she was a threat. She hoped Tyler picked up on the reference.

"What's the plan?" Tyler asked.

"Same as a hundred years ago. The elders and I fabricated a new barrier from the feathers of Thunderbirds." Jeni saw Tyler's eyebrows disappear under his hair. When his eyes met hers, she shook her head and he let Nik finish speaking. "Jeni will influence the monster with the thunderstone; draw him into its former prison. Then we'll set the barrier."

Jeni poked her head between the seats. "What about the guardians?"

"Guardian," Nik corrected her. "Me."

She gasped.

"If Ice arrives, you must not tell him I intend to stay in the cave." Nik met Jeni's eyes. "He'll no doubt argue, and there'll be no time to hesitate."

Jeni found herself unable to protest under his unwavering stare. Her head started to shake back and forth, but she heard herself choke out, "I won't tell Ice." She tore her eyes from his and looked down at the floor.

"I wish I had more time with him, but Ice will make a fine medicine man," Nik said quietly.

A sudden crack of lightning made them all look out the windows as a rumble vibrated the truck.

"The storm is close. If we want the aid and protection of the Thunderers, we have to go," Nik said.

"But..." Jeni looked to the drive, willing Ice's Jeep to appear around the corner. "We don't have the thunderstone."

"I brought one. The effect will not be as profound, but it's not without power." Nik looked into Jeni's eyes. "Especially in your possession."

Jeni's pulse picked up its pace. She had no idea if she could do what Nik wanted. She dug through her purse, slipping anything she thought would be useful into her pockets. Tyler opened the back of his car and rummaged around. When Jeni got out, he handed her a flashlight. "What's all this about Thunder? Birds... stones?"

Jeni explained as they followed Nik to the boat ramp, not really caring how outlandish it all sounded. But Tyler didn't make any smart comments, and there was no further conversation after they fell into a single-file line and made their way down the shoreline.

✺ ✺ ✺

Ice blinked as lightning flared directly in his line of sight. The accompanying clap of thunder resonated in his chest. His speed was way too fast for the park road, but he doubted anyone would be out when the sky threatened to let lose a deluge at any minute.

He skidded into the boat launch drive, praying his assumptions were correct. His headlights caught Nik's truck and he let out a whoop. In seconds he was parked and hanging over the seat to grab what he needed to take with him.

Ice was outside when he finally noticed the silver car parked on the other side of the pick-up.

Tyler's.

A barrage of emotions hit him all at once: surprise, happiness, worry, anticipation, fear…

A new burst of urgency spurred him to the lake. The sky lit up and he took advantage of the moment to study the shoreline. He was already picking his way over the rocky beach when the resulting rumble sounded. Even without the thunderstone, Nik wouldn't pass up the opportunity to face the manitou in a storm like this. Ice didn't know what the medicine man planned to do; he just hoped he got there in time to help.

The land on his right rose and soon became a steep embankment. Ice trained his light in that direction until the terrain grew treacherous and he needed to illuminate the ground in front of him. He stopped occasionally to sweep the bank with the beam.

He didn't expect to catch Nik and the others outside—he'd have to find the cave himself. If he missed the opening, he'd spend precious time backtracking.

And he was already late.

Too late?

The storm hung directly overhead; each brilliant blaze like an old-fashioned flashbulb. Ice's eyes were in a state of constant adjustment. Between claps of thunder, all he heard was the swooshing of leaves and the wind rushing past his ears.

The shore leveled out and widened. The bank on his right dropped quickly as he moved forward. He paused and flashed his light side-to-side in front of him.

He'd reached the beach. Somehow he'd missed the cave.

Swearing out loud, he retraced his steps.

He wished he had a clue or landmark—or at least a way to let someone know he was out here.

He pulled his cell phone from his pocket and prayed for a signal. Jeni, for sure, would have her phone with her.

Angrily Ice flipped the phone shut—it was useless tonight.

If only he'd been able to master the mental link with Nik. It worked when Nik used it—there was an "open line"—why couldn't Ice tap into it?

He was back to picking across rocks with the embankment high to his left. The cave had to be in this area. Ice stopped and closed his eyes. He evoked Nik's image, fleshing it out, filling in—

Something hit him hard from above. Knocked off his feet, Ice catapulted toward the ground. In the few seconds before he landed, he twisted sideways, arms clutched protectively over his abdomen. The side of his face slammed against a rock, exploding pain throughout his head.

Blackness was a welcome alternative.

...everything on the earth has a purpose,
every disease an herb to cure it,
and every person a mission.
This is the Indian theory of existence.

—*Mourning Dove, Salish*

CHAPTER 15

W hat's taking Nik so long?" Tyler glanced down the subterranean passage where Nik had retreated.

Already worried, the creases in Jeni's forehead deepened. "I don't know."

"Tie faster."

"Believe me; I'm going as fast as I can. I can't wait to get out of here." Jeni was trying to concentrate on what she was doing and not think about the cave or the darkness pressing in on the beams of their flashlights.

As they'd followed Nik into the cave, she noticed Tyler stealing glances in her direction. She steeled herself for some snide comment that would make her regret admitting her phobias, but he never said a word.

The passage wasn't too bad at first. It was wide, and tall enough that Tyler—who must be over six feet—had no issue walking upright. And with the large opening behind them, the cave wasn't completely black. Eventually though, they'd rounded a bend, and claustrophobia started to gnaw at Jeni's nerves.

Tyler had his arms wrapped around a rolled bundle, holding it while Jeni fastened ties to an ancient framework carved from the stone ceiling. He repositioned a hand out of her way. "How did Nik even hear Ice? I didn't hear anything."

"I think it's a medicine man thing. He heard Ice in his head—not with his ears."

Tyler shifted on his feet and rolled his eyes. "Telepathy?"

Jeni shrugged. The way Nik rushed out, saying he thought Ice was trying to contact him, had her worried. The fire smoldering in her stomach burned hotter and hotter as more time passed without Nik's return.

"Here," Jeni said, passing Tyler a long piece of rawhide. "You don't need to hold the barrier up anymore, just tie this around the roll so it doesn't flop down. Go check on Nik. I only have two ties left; I'll be right behind you."

Tyler studied her. "We should probably stay together."

"It's okay Tyler. Really." Right now she was more concerned about Ice and Nik than the surrounding darkness.

He took the hide and wrapped it around the bundle, moving deliberately. By the time he had it knotted, Jeni was on the last tie. "Go. I'll be a minute behind you."

Tyler hesitated and then nodded.

Jeni hurried with the last knot. Now that she was

alone, the blackness seemed to close in around her. She could sense the hollowness of the large chamber in front of her.

The underwater monster's prison.

The sizeable cavern housed a pool in the center covered by a solid stone ceiling. The walls consisted of stone interspersed with hard packed earth. Their earlier inspection of the area had revealed an opening in the far wall—a hole about two or three feet in diameter.

Tyler had no qualms about striding around the pool for a closer examination, and he'd reported that the tunnel beyond was not much larger than the opening, although big enough to crawl through on hands and knees. "You wouldn't get very far," Tyler reported, "it's caved in after about five feet."

Nik surmised that the tunnel might be how the monster's lackey had entered the chamber in order to destroy the barrier and the guardians to free Mishebeshu. When Jeni asked why the person wouldn't have come the way they did, Nik explained that the passage opening had been blocked with boulders and overgrown by vines and scrub grass. The first night he'd found it, the entrance looked as though it'd been ripped open, the surrounding rock marked with copper—the manitou had forced its way out.

Jeni let out a heavy breath. She was done.

She swept the beam of her light across the rolled bundle secured to the cave's ceiling. About a dozen rawhide ties anchored the barrier to what Nik call the 'framework' —a row of stone eyelets carved over a hundred years ago. When the hide that secured the roll was cut, the barrier would drop and cover the entrance to the chamber beyond.

Though the bundle resembled a thick woven blanket, it wasn't made of merely fabric and thread. The elders had constructed the barrier by incorporating every thunderbird feather available into the woven material.

"It's a simple plan," Nik had explained. "When we're ready, we'll go outside on top of the embankment. Jeni will call the manitou using the thunderstone. Assuming that works, I'll follow the creature inside and release the curtain—barring its path back out. Then we'll collapse the opening so no one can stumble in accidentally."

"Collapse?" Tyler asked. Nik reached into his pocket and handed Tyler what looked like a stick of dynamite. "See if you can find a hole or divot in the wall about halfway back to stick this in." But before Tyler could do that, Nik said Ice called him. He quickly showed Tyler and Jeni how to fasten the barrier to the framework and then hurried outside.

Jeni trained her light on a stone anchor without a tie.

"Shoot, missed one."

She told Tyler she'd be right behind him. She should at least check to see what was going on outside—she could come back for the last tie.

Jeni turned away and then paused. She took a deep breath. It was just one tie.

She picked up a length of hide and quickly looped and knotted it. Then she gathered up the remaining rawhide and stuffed it into the duffle Nik used to carry the barrier. With the bag zipped and on her shoulder, she scanned the ground with her light. If she grabbed everything, no one would have to come back in here. The beam fell on Nik's medicine bag so she picked it up and hurried down the passage.

* * *

Ice groaned and cracked his eyelids to the sight of a dirty pair of boots. He shifted his gaze and surveyed the man standing over him. A large boulder in the man's hands obstructed the lower half of his face. As Ice's muddled brain fought to make sense of the scene, he wondered if he'd already been hit with the rock or if he was about to be hit with the rock.

Oddly though, the man stared across the water, as if mesmerized. Ice heard agitated waves slapping at the sand and attempted to glance in that direction, but the rocky ground eclipsed his line of sight. He needed to move. If he could move.

When the man took a step backward, Ice flinched and rolled onto his back, his arms instinctively raised to protect his head. His assailant, however, merely dropped the boulder, his gaze still fixed on the lake. Pushing up onto his elbows, Ice studied the roiling water. This time he found what held the man's attention—two horns appeared between swells then disappeared behind the next wave. As alarm blossomed in his chest, Ice detected movement from the corner of his eye, and he turned to see Nik charging the man. Seconds before they collided, Ice's attacker spotted the medicine man and turned toward the embankment, scrambling for something to grasp.

Nik lunged for the man, who clutched a tree root and pulled himself over the lip of the bank, legs dangling. Defying his age, Nik jammed his foot into the loose, sandy dirt and leaped upward, catching his adversary's ankle and jerking it hard.

Ice struggled to get up, but waves of double vision forced him back down. He kept one eye on the water and the other on Nik. Fueled by desperation, the man had actually dragged Nik up the slope while pulling himself forward. The medicine man clung stubbornly, unable to secure a foothold.

Ice rolled onto his hands and knees, sparing a glance over his shoulder. The manitou's massive head protruded from the water, moving toward shore. Ice dragged himself toward the embankment, contemplating how he might be able to help Nik.

In a last effort at freedom, the man rammed his foot squarely into the medicine man's chest. Nik lost his grip and flew backwards. "No!" Ice shouted. He watched helplessly as Nik's body plummeted to the rocks below. The sharp snap of breaking bone tore a strangled moan from Ice's throat. He pressed his back against the bank and shifted his numb stare to check the progress of the underwater monster.

A blaze of lightning lit the lake with a tremendous crack. The manitou flailed, throwing itself back in the water.

The Thunderers had joined the battle.

Ice's reflexes screamed at him to go to Nik, but he fought the urge and pressed his head against the cold earth. Tears welled in his eyes. The apprentice hadn't missed the way his teacher's neck wrenched along with the terrible snapping sound; Ice feared Nik was beyond help. To go to the medicine man, he would expose himself to the assailant above and Ice was in no condition to fight. Raising his hand to the lump rising on his temple, he wished it would rain—the cool rain might help clear his head. He wiped his eyes on his sleeve and mustered the strength to stand.

Upright and braced against the steep slope, Ice noticed light flickering at the mouth of the cave. He had no idea if the guy who decked him was watching from above, but he didn't want anyone else ambushed. He picked up a small stone and waited. The light went out and a shadowy form emerged from the opening.

Tyler.

Ice tossed the rock and hit him on the arm. When Tyler looked his way, Ice put his finger to his lips and pointed upward. Tyler nodded, side-stepped, then nearly fell. Ice watched him crouch down and grapple with something.

Using the embankment for support, he edged over to Tyler, straining to see what the problem was. It looked as though Jeni's cousin was running his hand along a tree root, following it up the bank. Before he could ask, Tyler put his hand over his flashlight and turned it on.

Ice's eyes widened, realizing what had tripped Tyler. Wire.

With his light, Tyler traced the path of the wire up and around the cave entrance. He looked at Ice just as a flash of lightning lit the area and his eyes bugged out. "Whoa, what happened to you?"

"Blindsided."

"Where's Nik?"

Ice's chin sunk to his chest and he shook his head. Then he motioned toward Nik's body. Tyler must've been able to make out the medicine man's limp form because his face hardened. "Is the dude up there?" He pointed up the slope.

"He was, don't know if he still is."

"Well, it looks like he wired the cave to explode."

"Explode? Where's Jeni? Inside?" Ice was already trying to push past Tyler.

"Yeah. She should be out any minute." Tyler grabbed Ice's elbow and looked him directly in the eyes. "Keep her safe. I'll bet this is the same guy who tried to kill us. I'm going after the bastard."

Ice nodded.

When the darkness swallowed Tyler, Ice moved in front of cave. The next flash of lightning revealed Tyler's form climbing the bank. He glanced into the cave entrance and saw a faint glow. Good. Jeni was on her way out.

Ice stood no more than ten feet from Nik's body. He had to know if the medicine man was still alive. Gusts of wind continually brushed the leaves on the trees together, making it impossible to hear what might be happening in the forest above. Tentatively, he backed toward Nik's body, alternately watching his footing, scanning the forest, and keeping an eye on the cave opening.

He dropped to a crouch next to Nik, reached out

for his wrist, and pressed his thumb to the inside flesh.

A noise behind him made his blood run cold.

The sound of an aluminum canoe being dragged ashore.

Except Ice knew it wasn't a canoe.

* * *

Jeni directed her flashlight down the dark passage. She approached the curve warily. Increasing trepidation fought with her urgency to leave this place; she was certain something had gone terribly wrong outside.

"Tyler?" she called in a loud whisper as she rounded the bend. "Nik?"

Although her light didn't reach the opening ahead, she could detect a shadow, blacker than the grey hole. She breathed a sigh of relief and quickened her pace.

"No! No!" Someone shouted.

Jeni was about to break into a run when the beam of her light glinted off of something metallic.

"Jeni! No!"

She recognized Ice's voice and stopped dead in her tracks. Her flashlight illuminated the head of the monster in terrible clarity. Its eyes examined her with malevolence, as if it knew her purpose here. Scales grated the rock wall as the creature leisurely padded forward.

She stood, frozen, watching it stalk her. Then her eyes rose and focused between its horns, where Ice's form hovered; prey caught in the sights of a gun.

Except she was the prey.

And Ice held up a weapon.

She wanted to run. What was Ice waiting for?

A crack of lightning answered her question. The creature cringed and in the illuminated entrance Jeni saw Ice draw his arm back and throw. She watched the object fly end over end along the monster's back. Dropping everything, she rushed to catch it.

The lightning terminated, leaving Jeni blind. Reaching to where she imagined the object might be, she opened her hands. A hard surface grazed her left palm before Jeni heard a smash followed by the scatter of broken pieces.

Thunder boomed and she snatched her light from the ground. The creature remained frozen in place. Jeni swept her light over the floor of the cave, confused.

The ground was littered with rocks. What did Ice throw?

Wait. She trained her light on a tube-shaped rock.

Of course, the thunderstone!

She scrambled for every piece of stone in that odd shape until she heard the metallic scratching resume. Dumping the handful of rocks into her jacket pocket, she turned and fled into the cave knowing there was nowhere to hide.

Ducking under the rolled barrier, Jeni paused in the cavern opening. She side-stepped and pressed herself to the wall, her heart pounding wildly. She wondered if a broken thunderstone did her any good. She didn't even know how to control the monster.

Was she supposed to shout commands to it or make mental suggestions?

She turned off the flashlight.

Underwater lynx. Feline. Did that mean it could see in the dark?

Too many questions. Too much she didn't know.

Her breath came in short, ragged bursts as the sound of metal scraping dirt and stone grew louder. Her thoughts raced. *A simple plan. A simple plan.*

Maybe it could still work.

Jeni slipped the flashlight in one pocket while reaching into the other to gather the largest pieces of thunderstone. She gripped them tightly. Then, she slid her empty hand beneath her raincoat and into her back pocket. She curled her fingers around her pocketknife and drew it out.

The sound emanating from the passage changed in pitch and Jeni pictured the monster rounding the bend. She opened her pocketknife.

The cave went silent.

No, that wasn't true. She could hear the creature snuffling at the opening to the cavern.

Tears leaked out of the corners of her eyes and she clamped her mouth shut, terrified she might let out a whimper. She gripped the stones tighter in an effort to steady her trembling arm.

Here goes nothing.

Closing her eyes, she willed the spirit to the pool in the center of the large chamber. It was a water creature. Surely it wanted to get back in the water.

She thought about the feel of cool water on hot skin in the summertime. The silkiness of currents surrounding your body. The relief of rinsing away abrasive sand and dirt.

Jeni heard the creature slink forward, and pictured it slithering into the water. The thought that it would sniff her out presented itself and she desperately pushed it away.

She repeated her mantra: cool water, silky currents, cleansing liquid…willing the spirit to forget all else.

It continued to creep. Jeni nearly sobbed out loud when she heard the splash of the first paw. Breathing through her nose, her lips pressed together, she poured all of her will into the stone.

When her ears detected the lumbering body sinking into the water, she stepped sideways, feeling for the framework with her open knife still clutched in her fist. Her trembling hand followed the carved rock up and over the feather barrier. She felt for the rawhide Tyler had used to truss it.

Slipping the knife under the string, she blindly sawed while straining to hear any sign that the creature had changed its mind and was coming back. Suddenly, her hand flew up and the curtain fell as the hide gave way.

She spun and fled, fumbling for her flashlight, expecting to see someone—anyone—coming to find her. Finally, light on, she rounded the bend and began to run flat out.

In Jeni's mind, the terrific flash and boom computed as thunder and lightning so she didn't slow. There was a moment of confusion as she was pummeled by hurtling rocks and debris; then everything went black.

There is no death, only a change of worlds.
                              —*Chief Seattle, Suquamish*

Don't be afraid to cry. It will free your
mind of sorrowful thoughts.
                              —*Don Talayesva, Hopi*

CHAPTER 16

Jeni dragged herself up to hands and knees, disoriented and confused. The flashlight, still lit but barely visible in the haze, lay a few feet away. She retrieved it and swept the beam through the dust-clogged air. Coughing, she put her arm up to her face, breathing through her sleeve.

Who lit the dynamite?

Didn't they realize she was still inside?

Illuminated by her light was an enormous pile of rubble: rocks, earth, and tree roots.

In the settling dust it was impossible to see more than a few feet in front of her. She shuffled away from the debris, and as the passage curved, her brain cleared and processed her situation. An acid feeling of dread bloomed in her gut.

In denial, she peered down the passage and

when the feather barrier appeared in the glow of her flashlight, she confirmed what she already knew.

She was trapped.

Her heart sped up and the ball of dread exploded into full-blown terror.

She was imprisoned inside the cave with the monster!

Heading back the way she'd just come and jogging now, Jeni rounded the bend, desperately shining her light everywhere.

What was she looking for? Another way out?

She laughed crazily. The panicked sound scared her even more.

She needed to get a grip.

A rumble reverberated throughout the cave and Jeni froze, sweeping the beam of her flashlight around the passage, expecting more falling debris.

Nothing.

She drew in a shaky breath. Ice for sure knew she was in here.

Why hadn't he come after her?

He would get her out. She just didn't know how long it would take.

Or how long the batteries in her flashlight would last.

Jeni shuddered at the thought of complete blackness. Even so, the biggest concern was the manitou. Her hand drifted to the pocket full of pieces of thunderstone.

She had no idea if she'd controlled the creature or if she'd just gotten lucky.

For her own sanity, she had to believe she was

in control because the only thing between her and the monster was the barrier.

A woven blanket.

Made of feathers.

*　*　*

Raindrops splattering on his face jarred Ice from his stupor. No, not rain—Tyler stood over him, fingers dripping. He extended his hand and Ice grasped it, his head swimming as he came to a sitting position. Ice blinked in confusion.

Tyler's face was dirt-smeared and he used his sleeve to blot a bloody lip. "That guy won't be bothering us anymore." His eyes darted around, taking in the state of the surrounding area and his forehead creased. "Where's Jeni?"

Ice looked toward the cave.

It was gone.

He scrambled to his feet, disoriented.

"Where's Jeni?" Tyler repeated.

Ice spun in a circle. Nothing looked right. He stumbled down the shoreline a few feet trying to get his bearings. Lightning flashed, making him squint for a moment. "The cave," he choked out. "What happened?"

"That idiot had a detonator and blew the cave before I decked him," Tyler growled loudly over the thunder, then grabbed Ice's arm in desperation. "Tell me Jeni's not in there." He pointed to the jumble of debris.

Ice's eyes widened in horror as memories flooded his brain and events clicked into place. Jeni, the thunderstone, the beast's tail catapulting him into the embankment.

Tyler must've read the answer in his eyes. "Are you telling me she's trapped in that cave?"

"It's worse than that," Ice mumbled. "The manitou is in there with her."

"WHAT?"

But Ice was already at the pile of rubble. He began hurtling rocks, sticks and stones in every direction. "She was coming...saw her light...Mish...the manitou...I didn't hear it until it was too late...it was already inside before I could warn her. I threw her the stone. Then...it hit me. Oh God, we've got to get her out!"

Tyler had already joined him and they worked feverishly at the blockage. "Is Nik okay?" Tyler asked.

"I don't know," Ice's voice was grim as he glanced in the medicine man's direction and then back at the debris. Lightning lit the scene. They'd made minimal headway. "If it starts raining, this will be impossible," he muttered.

"We need help or tools," Tyler said. "I know where I can get a shovel pretty quick."

Ice nodded.

Tyler climbed the bank and was gone.

Ice angrily blinked tears from his eyes. Jeni would be okay.

She had to be.

THUNDERSTONE

* * *

Jeni sunk to the ground, her back against the cold, stone wall. She drew her knees up and wrapped her arms around them. The sobs she'd so far managed to hold at bay bubbled up from deep inside and she hung her head and let them go.

Ironically, despite everything that went wrong, Nik's simple plan had come to fruition. Jeni coaxed the monster into its prison, the barrier was in place, and the entrance collapsed.

Only instead of Nik, Jeni remained inside—positioned to act as guardian.

Destiny finds you.

Is that what this had been all about? Had she been drawn here to fulfill her fate?

Screw fate! She didn't want this.

Jeni rested her forehead on her knees, breathing in hiccupy breaths, tears soaking into her jeans.

She'd wanted to help, wanted to fix what she'd screwed up—make it right. Well she'd succeeded, right?

Things happen for a reason.

At least she'd met Ice; known him even for a short time. She reached for the painted stone hanging from her neck. Her fingers rubbed the cool surface and she thought about the picture painted on it.

Itasca.

Jeni could really sympathize with her right now. Here she was, trapped below the earth, sobbing. She wondered if Itasca had loved a man before she was forced to become the bride of the ruler of the underworld. That would make her sad story even more tragic.

She heard a rumble and this time, as the ground vibrated, Jeni realized it was thunder. She found a tissue in her pocket and blew her nose. Crying had helped clear the dust from her eyes and nose, though the dirty, mineral taste clung to the back of her throat. She leaned her head back against the wall, one hand still clutching the painted stone like a talisman, the other curled around the broken shards of thunderstone.

A soft, fluttering sound made Jeni sit up straight. She flicked her light in the direction of the noise. Movement caught her eye and she breathed a sigh of relief when she spied an owl perched on the pile of rubble. It closed its eyes and shied away from her light.

"Wher—" Jeni coughed and cleared her throat. "Where did you come from?"

The owl flew a ways down the passage.

Jeni traced its path with her light.

Was it in here when the entrance blew up? Had to be.

It fluttered a little farther away.

Unless there was another way in and out of here? With nothing to lose, Jeni rose and followed the owl.

When she was in sight of the feather barrier, she stopped. The owl ducked around the obstacle and flew into the cavern.

"Sister." The voice came from nowhere and everywhere.

Jeni gasped, shining the flashlight around her.

She frowned. Was it a trick? Was the manitou trying to lure her to the other side of the barrier?

She stood perfectly still for what seemed like a long time. The only sound she heard was the impatient fluttering of the owl. She stepped close to the barrier and peeked around it. Her light reflected off the undisturbed surface of the pool.

Convinced she'd imagined the voice, Jeni directed the beam around the large space and eventually found the owl, perched in the hole across the chamber.

"You seek guidance?" The voice came from right beside her and Jeni jumped, swinging her light to the left and retreating until her back was against the wall. She stared, wide eyed, at the specter in front of her.

The Indian girl looked to be about Jeni's age. Her jet-black hair hung loose over a hide tunic. She smiled gently at Jeni. "You're not sure what role you play."

Jeni was speechless, and amazed to find she wasn't afraid. Contrary to her smile, the girl's eyes reflected a profound sadness. She sat and motioned for Jeni to do the same.

When Jeni was seated cross-legged across from her, the girl regarded her, eyebrows raised.

Jeni asked the question most pertinent to the girl's statement. "Is it my destiny to be the guardian?"

"It is true that you have met with destiny here, priestess." The girl put emphasis on the last word. "Although whether this is your first walk with spirits or your last, is up to you."

"But without a guardian…"

"The soul of the guardian must be given freely." The girl's eyes took on a hard edge. "But much like me, you have been captured; trapped against your will by the designs of a selfish god." She put her fingertips on her chest. "I, for his desire." Her hands extended to Jeni. "You, for his vengeance."

She sighed, eyes downcast. "Whatever his reason, it is ultimately about power: exerting it, displaying it, or acquiring it."

Jeni shook her head slightly. "I don't understand."

"Forgive me. This is what you need to know. To be the guardian, you must want to stay here—if that is your choice, it will save your soul. Should you merely die here, you give in to the quest for vengeance. Your soul will fuel the force that seeks you and yours."

Jeni opened her mouth but the girl held up a hand to silence her. "You have a third choice—life. Save yourself, warn my people that the underwater manitou is not under guard, and go on to become that which you are destined to be."

"Save myself?" Jeni asked.

The girl nodded. "There is a new spark in your heart to which you have pinned your hopes, but awaiting rescue would be your demise. With no guardian, once the Thunderers have gone, the barrier will no longer contain Mishebeshu. Only by facing your deepest fears will you find salvation."

The girl stopped to contemplate a distant roll of thunder. "You have much to think about and little time to make a choice: life, death, or guardianship." She stood. "Choose wisely." With sorrowful eyes, the girl smiled at Jeni and backed out of the flashlight's glow.

Jeni directed the light down the passage and her

head reeled with disorientation. She expected to see the corridor leading back to the blockage; instead her light fell on the pile of rocks and rubble.

Jerking the light all around her, Jeni realized she was sitting in the same spot she'd been when she sat down and cried.

Had she ever left?

Another roll of thunder, quieter this time.

The significance of seeing an owl was not lost on Jeni.

Did she have a vision?

Her hand still clutched the stone at her throat.

Itasca. Had to be—the girl said she'd been trapped here by a selfish god.

Considering the events of the past few days, Jeni didn't find it too hard to believe Itasca might visit her in a vision. Right now, she was willing to go on a little faith.

Jeni wished she had the courage to choose guardianship, to accept a noble and honorable death. To be honest, it wasn't just courage she lacked—it was certainty. She believed in her heart she had more to do— that the events here were just the tip of the iceberg.

She'd only just begun to find out who she was.

So, if she couldn't be the guardian and didn't want her soul taken in vengeance, she had to get out of here. Itasca was right; Jeni counted on Ice to come to the rescue. But it wasn't up to him.

It was up to her.

By facing her deepest fears.

Jeni looked around.

Wasn't she already surrounded by her fears?

Trapped in a dark, closed space?

Thunder rumbled again—muffled.

"With no guardian, once the Thunderers have gone, the barrier will no longer contain Mishebeshu." Itasca's words reminded her she was running out of time and she rose to her feet. If she waited here, she'd be trapped; at the monster's mercy. Jeni set off down the passage, stopping to retrieve Nik's medicine bag.

She knew where she had to go. What was scarier than where she was now?

Somewhere smaller.

And blacker.

Power comes from the heart...
your head will run away from you,
but your heart is always with you.

—*Curly Bear Wagner, Blackfoot*

CHAPTER 17

Where in the world was Tyler with that shovel? Ice wiped his forehead with his arm, trying to see into the forest above. He was getting nowhere without tools.

He trotted over to Nik, who remained in the same limp pose on the rocks. Ice lifted his hand and felt for a pulse. Weak, but still there. Fresh blood trickled from behind the medicine man's head.

"Nik." Ice wanted to get Nik off the rocks, but was afraid to move him, not knowing the extent of his injuries. Ice slipped out of his jacket and t-shirt, putting the jacket back on. After soaking the shirt in the lake, he pressed it to the medicine man's forehead. "Nik, hey Nik." He brought the cloth over both cheeks, hoping the cold water would rouse his teacher.

To his surprise, it hadn't rained yet. Judging by the diminishing rumbles of thunder, the storm was taking its bloated clouds elsewhere.

After a second trip to the water, Ice was rewarded when he applied the cloth to Nik's head. The medicine man's eyes fluttered and opened. He focused on Ice's face.

"Ice. You're okay. What happened?"

"You got launched off the bank and hit the rocks hard. I didn't want to move you. What can you feel?"

"Rocks."

Humor. That was a positive sign.

"Can you wiggle your toes?"

Nik moved his feet and hands. He braced himself to sit.

"Wait. Try moving your head first—carefully."

With a grimace, the medicine man slowly lifted his head. "Ouch. Is there a rock or stick or something jammed in my neck?"

Ice bent down and directed his flashlight behind Nik's head. "Can you lift this shoulder?" He set the light on the rocks and used both hands to help Nik roll slightly on his side. He breathed a sigh of relief. Now he knew what the awful crack was when Nik hit the ground. "One of the long beads on your necklace broke and impaled the base of your neck. Luckily, it went sideways into the trapezoid muscle."

"Well pull it out then," Nik replied, irritation spiking his tone. "Where are the others?"

"Things haven't gone well." Ice scrunched up his face—the blood and guts part of being a medicine man was his least favorite part. "Hang on." He took his shirt and rinsed it one more time in the lake. Then he gave the light to Nik to hold, adjusting the older man's arm until he held it correctly. Ice began catching Nik up on the events of the night.

Pressing down on the wound with the wet shirt,

he yanked the shard of bead out as quickly as possible and then covered it with the cloth to stem the bleeding.

Nik merely grunted. "I'm going to have a nice lump on my head to go with this," he said, giving the light to Ice and holding the shirt to his neck.

"I have no idea what's happened to Tyler," Ice continued. "He went for a shovel; I assumed it was close by." He scanned the forest above them. "He said he took care of the guy who attacked us, but he's been gone a while."

Nik looked out at the sky over the lake. "Jeni is inside with the manitou?"

Ice nodded and followed Nik's gaze.

The sky was clearing.

*** *** ***

Jeni peeped around the feather barrier. With her hand over the lens, she directed the light into the cavern, careful not to shine it directly into the water. The surface was still.

She moved her fingers to let out a bit more light and examined the hole in the back wall. Once she skirted her way around the pool undetected, she would have to hoist herself into the tunnel. The opening looked to be three to four feet off the ground.

Jeni noticed the light wavering and realized her hands were shaking. Somehow she had to work up the courage to enter the chamber.

She barely heard the next rumble of thunder. The

impossibly remote sound was enough to spur her on.

Feathers tickled her face and neck as she slipped around the curtain, back pressed to the wall, breathing shallowly through her mouth. Shuffling sideways, Jeni made her way around the edge of the pool, never allowing her light to stray from the surface of the water. Her concentration was so intense that she stumbled into a rock and nearly lost her balance.

Teetering on one foot, she watched in horror as the stone she kicked rolled down the incline toward the water. Both feet were on the ground and she was frozen in place when it hit the water with a plop.

Her heart thumped double-time.

The rock sent ripples across the pool while Jeni held her breath. The cold of the cavern wall crept through her jacket and she shivered. Was it her imagination or were the ripples coming back this way?

She wasn't waiting to find out. On the move again, she alternated lighting the way in front of her and watching the pool. The world outside seemed to be silent—she hadn't heard thunder since she'd entered the cavern.

Reaching her destination, Jeni inspected the tunnel… so small… so dark. She turned to make a last sweep across the water with her light, and confirmed what her ears already told her—tiny waves gently lapped the shore. Her raspy breath seemed magnified by the spacious chamber.

She thought about the Would You Rather game she'd played with her friends. *Would you rather be trapped in a dark hole or be eaten by a dragon-like monster?*

Jeni knew she was losing it because a giggle rose

in her throat.

Nik's bag went through the hole first and she swung it to the back of the space, then swallowed the giggle and tossed her light in too.

As soon as the flashlight left her hand, she instantly regretted it. No way could she make herself climb into that little space. Wrapping her arms across her chest, Jeni stood looking into the hole as panic wormed its way from her chest to her brain.

No bleeping way.

She would go back to the blocked entrance and wait for Ice.

After she got her light back.

Putting her head, arms, and shoulders through the hole, she sprang off her feet and stretched forward, but her reach fell short.

Fabulous.

She hung for a moment on her stomach, her legs dangling on one side and her arms on the other. The ground was too far for her toes to push her up any further. She was about to drop back to her feet and try again, when she heard a sound behind her.

A gurgle.

The fear that surged through Jeni obliterated her panic. It burned with an unrelenting urgency, threatening to burst from inside her.

With nothing to grasp and pull herself through the opening, Jeni reached back and braced her hands on either side of the hole. She let out a strangled whimper and kicked wildly with her feet, pushing with her arms.

Fortunately, the laws of physics came to the

rescue. Once she'd dragged her torso through to her hips, she leaned forward and stretched her arms way out in front of her. Her body's center of gravity shifted and she slid through the hole and into the tunnel.

She pulled her legs up under her and scrambled as far as she could get from the opening. At first the only sound she could hear was her own panting and her heart thumping wildly, but eventually she detected the sound of water in motion.

She knew when the creature broke the surface because the soft swirling, gurgling noise changed to splashing, along with waves sloshing against the shore. Snatching the flashlight, she switched it off. The sound of metal grating on stone crawled up her spine, and she shuddered.

The monster must've paused at the feather barrier. Jeni heard nothing for a long, agonizing interval as she fought to keep her ragged breathing under control. The warm dampness of tears streaked her cheeks, and she closed her eyes against the darkness.

After an indeterminable span of time, a ripping sound made her jump. A new noise joined in, something under strain. Jeni pictured the manitou's horns impaled into the feather barrier as it tore the binding holding it in place. She heard a snap, crack, and another snap, and then the scraping grew less pronounced as the creature rounded the corner. It would be back, though, once it found the passage to the water was blocked.

She turned on her light, blinking her tears away so she could study the wall of dirt behind her. Tyler was right; it looked fresh—loose. Jeni pawed through

Nik's bag until she found a flat piece of—rock? shell?—and began frantically scraping at the dirt. It wasn't easy. Her tool was small and so was the space. She continually had to use her feet to kick the dirt behind her.

A bellow echoed throughout the cavern and Jeni froze in fear, quickly switching off her light. She sat trembling, listening to the monster return to the cavern and cry again.

The manitou knew it was trapped, and it was pissed.

Afraid to turn the light on, Jeni attacked the wall of dirt. As the earth mounded behind her, she eventually comprehended what was happening.

She was burying herself alive!

Wouldn't death by monster be preferable? Less torturous?

The thought made her incapable of digging further and her eyes again filled with tears.

Please. I don't want to play this game anymore. I wouldn't rather...

Again, the sound of metal scratching dirt.

Jeni clawed at the wall, not sure when the tears spilled over and she began weeping in earnest. Her ears were filled with scratching, scraping, and her own sobs. Then the earth in front of her fell away, and hands grasped her arms.

She screamed and kicked, trying to pull away, but the arms came around her firmly.

"Jeni? Jeni! Hey, it's okay. It's okay."

She knew that voice.

She was dragged for a few feet until they emerged

into a dimly-lit space where Jeni was no longer fighting, but clinging, gulping in shuddering breaths of air. He let her calm down, brushing dirt from her hair and arms.

As her breathing regulated, Jeni realized she was in that stupid cellar again, she was okay and she was—

Ack!—clinging to her cousin.

Jeni let go of Tyler and sat back, looking anywhere but directly at him.

He stood. "Are you okay?"

"Uh…yeah…good…I'm good," Jeni stammered, brushing dirt off her legs.

Tyler extended his hand to help her up. "I can't believe I'm in this freaking cellar saving your butt again."

As she reached for his hand, her eyes flicked up and caught his lopsided grin.

She chuckled and his smile widened.

"C'mon," he said. "Let's get the hell out of here."

Love your life, perfect your life,
Beautify all things in your life.
Seek to make your life long, and its
purpose in the service of your people.

—*Chief Tecumseh, Shawnee*

CHAPTER 18

In the restroom of the Community Center, Jeni washed her face and managed to get most of the dirt from her clothes; she also dumped out her shoes. Then, with her head hanging upside down, she shook her fingers through her hair before brushing it. It was the best she could do without a shower.

She paused as she stepped into the meeting room, looking for Ice. Not many people occupied the tables, so he and Nik were easy to spot. Ice smiled and slid a can of pop in front of her as she slipped into the chair next to him. "I thought you might be thirsty."

"I am, thanks." Jeni popped the can open and took a long drink. Ice wore some kind of souvenir t-shirt that was one size too small. "New shirt?"

"Yeah." Ice rolled his eyes. "Thanks for noticing."

There was no way for Jeni not to notice the way it revealed every contour underneath. "How's your head?"

Ice's hand rose to the bandage on his temple.

"Fine, nothing time and ibuprofen won't fix."

"How about you?" Jeni asked Nik, who sat across the table.

"I'm sore, and I'm sure I'll take longer to heal than Ice, but I'll live."

Jeni scanned the room. "Where's Tyler?"

"He went with some guys back out to the park to tie up 'loose ends'," Ice said. "We needed someone who knew where to go and he volunteered."

"What I wondered," Nik said, "Is how Tyler knew the tunnel in the manitou's chamber led to the cellar."

"When Tyler and I were trapped in the cellar, we saw the collapsed tunnel," Jeni explained. "Then, when he chased that guy, that's where they ended up. He said he didn't really put it all together though, until he went back for the shovel and remembered what you said," she nodded toward Nik, "about the tunnel in the cavern being how the guy got in to free the manitou."

Jeni glanced at Ice. "Once he came to the conclusion they were one and the same, he started digging to get me out of the cave." She smiled. "Although he didn't expect to find me already in the tunnel."

"Why were you in the tunnel?" Nik asked.

On the way to the reservation, Jeni told Ice about her vision of Itasca, but Nik hadn't heard any of her story yet, so she filled him in. "I'm not sure what she meant about vengeance or something, 'seeking you and yours.' I pretty much got the rest of it though, and it's a good thing I got out of there because the under-water monster broke through the barrier as soon as the storm was gone. And he was not happy to find the entrance caved in."

After her final statement, Jeni's eyebrows rose. "Is that why the monster wants vengeance? Does it think I imprisoned it again?"

Nik took a moment to contemplate her question. "I don't think Itasca referred to the manitou seeking revenge. She likened your entrapment to her own and mentioned a selfish god. Mishebeshu is a demigod. The god she must have been talking about is Chebiabo."

"Is he the…?"

"Ruler of the underworld, remember?" Ice didn't look happy.

Fear prickled down Jeni's spine. She glanced worriedly at Nik and Ice as they exchanged a look.

Nik reached across the table as if to take Jeni's hand, paused, and placed his hand on her sleeve. "Don't forget the most important message: to become the person you're destined to be. Research your family's heritage, find out who you are." He sat back, flicked his eyes to Ice and then back to Jeni. "I'm sure you'll be in touch with Ice; let me know if I can help you."

"Thanks," Jeni said, and meant it. She intended to make good on all of the conditions included in the choice she'd made. Now, more than ever, she wanted to discover what kind of skeletons lurked in her family closet. "Will you pass on Itasca's warning about the manitou?"

Nik nodded. "Absolutely." He surveyed the room. "In fact, it looks like most of the elders are here;

I guess it's time I give them an update."

"What will you do now?" Jeni asked quickly. "About the monster, I mean."

Nik must've guessed her underlying question. "Don't worry, for now the manitou is physically trapped. Though the situation is temporary, it's bought us some time. We'll keep watch while we consult with neighboring tribes as well as the spirit world." He stood. His smile for Jeni was genuine. "Your obligation here has been fulfilled, but I have a feeling your role as a priestess has just begun."

Jeni watched him walk away and understood Ice's respect for Nik. His intuition, knowledge, and wisdom made him a force to be reckoned with.

Ice touched her shoulder and then pushed back his chair and stood up. "Come with me? I want to show you something."

She shot him a questioning look but got up and followed him.

They crossed the room to a sliding glass door covered by vertical blinds on the opposite side. Ice slid the door open and held the blinds aside for Jeni. She stepped through the doorway and Ice followed her, closing the door behind him.

Jeni's jaw dropped in awe. Unlike most sliding glass doors, this one didn't lead outside, instead, they stood in a room surrounded by glass. Floor to ceiling windows made up the three outside walls of the room. Beyond the small clearing outside the building, the Chippewa Forest loomed dramatically.

Ice motioned her over to the windows. "I love this room because it's like being outside," he said. "It's not used much in the winter because it's cold, so that's when I come out here the most. It's a great place to think."

Although Ice hadn't turned on any lights, the brightness of the room they'd left filtered through the blinds on the sliding glass door, allowing Jeni to make out the shadowy shapes of furniture. She made her way across the room, and as her eyes adjusted to the dimness, she recognized the kind of rattan sofa and chairs found in Florida rooms and screened porches.

Jeni stepped close to the windows and looked up at the sky. The dark clouds that had hung over Lake Itasca hovered above. "The storm followed us."

As if in confirmation, the sky lit up, triggering rumbles of thunder. "I never thought I'd feel good about a thunderstorm, but now it seems almost comforting," she said. "Like having a big dog around when you're home alone."

Ice chuckled softly. He moved behind her and slipped his arms around her waist.

Jeni leaned into him, resting her head on his chest, his warmth radiating through her. She didn't feel awkward, nervous, or scared.

She felt safe.

Her hands closed over his and their fingers interlaced.

An image flickered, but was so brief, no details materialized.

Lightning flashed, illuminating the room from all sides. The corresponding thunder cracked loudly, and wind rattled the windows.

"We should go," Ice murmured.

Jeni sensed his apprehension. Here they were, sequestered in this dimly-lit room, no safeguard. She knew his fight for self-control was beyond that of a typical teenager, yet she wasn't afraid of what he might do next or what his intentions were.

She trusted him.

Turning in the circle of his arms, she rose up on her toes to kiss him. Reluctant at first, Ice soon yielded and kissed her back.

When he drew away, Jeni studied the glacial blue of his eyes, and memorized his cheekbones and the way his hair trailed over his shoulders when he tilted his head down. She reached up and twined a piece through her fingers, wanting to remember everything about him.

Jeni didn't know how long they stood there kissing, barely aware that their intensity rivaled that of the storm outside. Then the clouds released the rain they'd been holding back for hours. The deluge of water hit the rooftop as if spilled from a giant bucket. In the room lined by windows, the roar was enormous. They both turned to look, and as water poured over the glass, the room appeared to be melting.

Ice's hands were hot on the small of her back and Jeni's thumbs stroked the nape of his neck. She turned back to him, chin lifted, but he slid his hands up and pressed her against his chest. "We can't stay here," he said, his voice low and raspy.

She wasn't ready to let him go.

Jeni could hear his heart thumping rapidly, and felt the slight tremor in his embrace. He was close—so close to losing control. If she didn't break away, whatever happened next would be her fault—not his.

She reluctantly withdrew her hands and took a half-step back. As his arms dropped away she caught his hands. "Ice, you said we'd work it out. Did you mean it?" She hadn't meant to sound so anguished, but the raw edge of her emotions was plain.

Her eyes welled up, and she looked down at their hands. Ice let go and raised her chin until she was staring into his eyes. "Yes." He wiped the corner of her eye gently with his thumb. "I mean it."

"How…when?"

"Soon. I can drive out—Michigan's not that far away."

"Ice—it's an entire state and a great lake away."

Ice chuckled. "I can manage—hey! I just thought of something." He took her hand and pulled her toward the door.

Jeni was relieved that no one noticed as they emerged from the small room. Although the roar of the rain wasn't as loud as in the glass room, the elders seemed intent on listening to Nik.

Ice led her to a hallway and stopped in front of a huge bulletin board. Finding the memo he wanted, he pointed to a list of cities. "Are any of these cities close to where you live?"

Jeni scanned the list. She recognized a lot of the names—they were cities all over Michigan. She pointed. "Southfield is probably about twenty minutes from my house," she said. "Why?"

"We put on Native American events in various places to teach others about our culture. One thing they always have is storytelling."

Jeni's eyes widened. "Are you the storyteller?"

"I could be. I'll volunteer and see if Nik will put in a good word for me. I'd be there for almost a week," he grinned.

"How soon?"

Ice traced his finger across the notice. "July. Next month!"

Jeni stepped forward and hugged him tightly. "Okay, a month. In the meantime we have phones and e-mail."

He laughed and put his arms around her, resting his chin on her head. "Looks like the elders finished talking to Nik. And Tyler's back."

Jeni turned and saw people getting up and milling about the room. Tyler sat at a table with a few guys who looked about his age. When she and Ice approached, Tyler's eyebrow twitched as he considered Jeni for a moment. "You guys just appeared out of nowhere."

A blush heated her cheeks, but she ignored his comment. "What did you do about that guy?"

"Well, apparently he came to after we left, and used a sharp edge on the furnace to saw through the ropes I used to tie him up."

"Wait a minute," Jeni interrupted. "He was in the cellar?"

"Yeah, after I knocked him out, I rolled him in and tied him up."

Jeni shuddered. In the dark and confusion, she hadn't noticed he was there when Tyler pulled her from the tunnel.

"Anyway," Tyler continued, "without anything

to push the door open, he couldn't get out. When he heard us coming, he must've crawled through the tunnel and hid in the cave. I bet he hoped we'd think he escaped."

Tyler exchanged a grin with one of the guys he was with. "The dude didn't fool anyone, though. Lee over there," he pointed across the table, "is an excellent tracker and knew exactly where the guy was hiding."

Lee crossed his arms over his chest and smiled.

"You know how he had the cave entrance rigged to blow up?" Tyler glanced at Ice, then continued without waiting for an answer. "Well, the cellar was wired too. We found the detonator." A grin spread across Tyler's face as he waited for a reaction.

"You blew up the cellar?" Jeni asked.

Tyler nodded, his grin even bigger.

"The guy's trapped in the cave with the underwater monster? Cool, I love poetic justice," Ice said.

Jeni stepped over by her cousin and clapped him on the shoulder. "Nice job."

"After what he did to us—believe me, it was a pleasure." Tyler drained the cup in front of him and checked his watch. "Whoa—it's later than I thought." He looked up at Jeni. "We should get going."

"What are you drinking?" Jeni wrinkled her nose. "You smell like alcohol."

Tyler flashed a huge smile. "Home brew. Stronger than I expected." He dug in his pocket and pulled out his car keys, holding them out to her. "Good thing you can drive us back."

She took the keys and rolled her eyes at him.

Barbara Pietron

"Yeah, good thing."

Ice gave Jeni directions back to the resort while walking with them to Tyler's car. Only drips and puddles remained from the storm. Even the wind had died down. Tyler got in the passenger seat, and Jeni and Ice stopped on the other side of the car.

Ice took his time kissing her goodbye, maybe to make sure it was vision-free, or maybe because it would be a month before he saw her again. Maybe both.

Then he opened the car door for her. "See you soon."

She smiled and climbed inside. "Promise?" She looked up at him.

He grinned. "Whether I'm the storyteller or not."

"Okay." She let him swing the door shut and started the car. While adjusting the seat and fastening her seatbelt, she watched Ice walk back to the community center. She shifted the car into reverse, but didn't back out until he was out of sight.

An uncomfortable silence hung between her and Tyler. Ever since they'd been trapped in the cellar together, their relationship embarked on unfamiliar territory.

"He's all right." Tyler's speech wasn't quite slurred, just slow.

"Yeah, he is." So, what—were they friends now?

"For a dude with a stupid name."

Or maybe not—maybe they were still rivals. "You realize he's Indian, right? His name is Shattered Ice."

"I guess that's a decent excuse."

Tyler's acquiescence surprised Jeni. She liked this

subdued and docile version of her cousin. She'd probably never get a better opportunity to say what she
wanted to say.

"Thanks for going with me tonight," she said
quietly. "And for believing me about the monster."

"Uh…I don't think I ever said that."

Jeni glanced sideways to see if he was joking,
but Tyler wore an impassive expression, his gaze
focused on a flat object he held on his lap. "What do
you mean?" she protested. "You took me to the state
park…to meet Nik and Ice."

"Right. But you were hell-bent on joining them
before I came along. You would've found a way to get
there." His tone wasn't argumentative; it was matter-
of-fact. He flipped the disk-shaped thing over and over
in his fingers. "I figured I either had to go with you to
make sure you were safe, or tell someone where you
were and what you were up to. But I could hardly tell
your parents I knew someone wanted to kill you now,
could I?"

Jeni gripped the steering wheel in disbelief.
"But…but…the barrier…you helped me…"

"Look, it's clear what Nik believes, and probably
Ice too. You yourself said you believe because they
believe, so I went along with an open mind. But the
injuries and destruction I saw tonight were the work
of one psychotic human being."

She shook her head. "No, Ice was knocked out by
the monster's tail."

"Ice most likely has a concussion because the
psycho slammed his head into a rock. He could barely
stand when I came out of the cave; he probably just

passed out." Tyler tossed the object up with one hand and caught it in the other. *Flick. Plop.*

Her mouth was open to spew out the next argument. If the monster hadn't chased her into the cave, she never would've been trapped. For that matter, what about the existence of the cave itself? And the deaths? What about... Jeni closed her mouth. Tyler would no doubt have a logical explanation to everything she offered. Because bottom line, he never saw the monster, ergo, it didn't exist.

Flick. Plop.

"What is that?" Jeni snapped. "Did you pick up a rock somewhere or something?"

"No." *Flick. Plop.* "Lee gave it to me."

Tyler held out the thing he'd been playing with. As they passed under a streetlight, a metallic glow flared off the object. For a moment, the image of the monster caught in the beam of her light flashed in Jeni's mind and she shuddered.

"Can I see it?" she asked as she coasted to a stop at a traffic light. She felt a slight tingle on her palm and a shiver crept up her arm though the disk was still warm from Tyler's hands. Her fingers tentatively explored what the dim lighting couldn't reveal.

The flat orb was slightly larger than her hand with a thickness that tapered from a half inch to about an eighth of an inch. A raised ridge ran along the thicker edge; the remaining surface scarred by deep gouges. The other side was remarkably smooth. As she slid her fingers along the gouges, Jeni imagined the cave entrance, marked with copper after the monster's escape.

"Did Lee tell you what this is?" Jeni asked casually. She passed the disk back to her cousin, breathing an inaudible sigh of relief when it left her hand.

"Copper. He said it would've been extremely valuable a long time ago but not so much anymore. He told me to keep it for good luck."

Copper. Just as she thought.

Suddenly Jeni wanted to scream with laughter. She could totally throw this in her cousin's face. Tyler held, in his hand, a scale from the very monster whose existence he denied. He may still refuse to believe it, but deep down he'd know. And Jeni would be right for a change.

Of course it would rekindle their rivalry.

Did she want that?

Truthfully? No. Jeni had to admit Tyler was a worthy ally—she'd rather be with him than against him.

Her next thought completely contradicted her inclination to keep her mouth shut and sent a chill down the back of her neck. They were cousins. They shared ancestry. Was it safe for Tyler to have a scale from the underwater manitou in his possession? After all, her innocent purchase of a statue had turned into a full-blown catastrophe.

She had to warn him, right?

Even if he didn't want to admit the truth?

Jeni drew in a breath but before she uttered a sound, Tyler spoke. And solved her conundrum.

"Since it's copper, I guess it'll eventually turn green."

Awesome. She'd just learned about this in

chemistry a few months ago. "You can put it in a zip bag to protect it. But most important…" Jeni paused to make sure he was paying attention.

Tyler looked at her and waved his hand in a "go on" gesture.

"Keep it away from any and all water."

A Note From the Author

Thanks for reading *Thunderstone,* Book One of the Legacy in Legend Series. I hope you'll consider reviewing it on Amazon.com. Reviews not only help readers make a good choice, they also increase the chance that Amazon will recommend the book to others. I would greatly appreciate it!

Need to know what happens next? Book Two of the Legacy in Legend Series, *Veiled Existence,* is available now at Amazon.com and other book retailers.

If you haven't already read the Legacy in Legend Prequel, *Heart of Ice,* you can get it FREE from my website: www.barbarapietron.com/freebies.

For the latest news about the Legacy in Legend Series and other novels, join my reader group at: www.barbarapietron.com/join-me. Members have exclusive access to all of the free content on my site, including a novel, novelette, short stories and other fun stuff.

I love to get to know my readers! You can email me at author@barbarapietron.com or connect with me at:

Facebook: facebook.com/barbara.pietron.19
Instagram: instagram.com/barbarapietron_author
Goodreads: goodreads.com/BarbP

Hope to hear from you! Happy Reading!

—*Barbara Pietron*

Acknowledgements

First I have to thank my husband, who made it possible for me to be a stay-at-home mom and writer. On the subject of getting published, he never said if; only when.

I am ever grateful to my daughter, Nikki Pietron, and sister, Judy Skemp, who graciously spent countless hours reading, re-reading, and offering advice to improve the story. Also, for everyone who took the time to read my manuscript, give me feedback, and encourage me to pursue my dreams: Lisa White, Jim White, Leslie Carnacchi, Sarah Ford, Kelly Nykanen, Betty Gerard, Bob Fulks, Jayne King, Claire Abell, Renee Wright, Nancy Hanes, Barb Neyens, Ann Skemp, and my mom, Jeannie Duehr—thanks guys, your support is everything when faced with stacks of rejections! Also, thank you to those who read my entry in the Amazon Breakthrough Novel Award contest and cheered me on; discovering such a wealth of believers strengthened my resolve to stay the course.

My dream would not be a reality had Leslie Carnacchi not referred me to Scribe Publishing Company where Jennifer Baum decided to take a chance on a debut author; a huge round of applause for Jennifer and the rest of the staff at Scribe Publishing.

I'd like to give credit to my favorite blog: misssnarksfirstvictim.blogspot.com for the critiques, links, advice, commiseration, and support from the Authoress herself as well and the community of writers that follow her blog. If you're an aspiring author, check it out.

Thank you to my niece, Cassie Pietron, for taking an author photo worthy of publication. You can find Cassie Pietron Photography on Facebook at: www.facebook.com/cassiepietronphotos

Last, but never least, I must thank my dad. Born and raised blocks from the Mississippi River, he travelled the world, but chose to return to the river for his last big adventure. Miss you Dad.

About the Author

Photo Credit: Cassie Pietron

Barbara Pietron has written two other books in the Legacy in Legend Series: a prequel, *Heart of Ice* and the second book, *Veiled Existence*. She is also the author of the stand-alone novel *Soulshifter*. In 2013, *Thunderstone* was awarded Book of the Year Finalist by *Foreword Reviews*.

When she's not writing, Barbara works in a library where she's tortured by all the books she has yet to read. She's a cult fan of the movies *Labyrinth* and *Nightmare Before Christmas* and a fan of all things Tim Burton. Barbara lives in Royal Oak, Michigan with her husband, daughter and a cat that often acts like a dog.

Get the Legacy in Legend prequel FREE at www.barbarapietron.com

Available at Amazon.com or your favorite book retailer, online and in stores